The MacOrvan Curse

The MacOrvan Curse

Florence Bowes

DOUBLEDAY & COMPANY, INC.

GARDEN CITY, NEW YORK

1980

All of the characters in this book
are fictitious, and any resemblance
to actual persons, living or dead,
is purely coincidental.

ISBN: 0-385-15844-0
Library of Congress Catalog Card Number 79–48086

*TO BILL, FOR THOSE YEARS OF
A VERY SPECIAL LOVE.*

The MacOrvan Curse

CHAPTER ONE

Castle MacOrvan, stronghold of the Clan MacOrvan, since Robert the Bruce created a barony in 1311, rose massive and forbidding atop the deep red rock cliffs of Mull, overlooking the curve of Loch na Keal. Blackened by the starless night and the ferocious December storm, the fortress, built of a natural blue-gray stone of Scotland, now appeared a thrusting, tortured extension of the dark crags below, scarred and sculptured by the ravenous appetite of the greedy sea. The incessant battering crash of the waves, meshing with the inhuman screaming of the wind, created a maniacal violence, as if all witches and warlocks were engaged in battles to the death.

Inside the castle all was silent, a heavy, unnatural silence broken only by thin whispers of the wind as it hissed its way around the slits of windows and under the enormous metal-bound door. Guttering flares, stuck in the walls, pointed the way up the spiral stone stairway to a large room hung floor to ceiling with tapestries to keep out the bitter cold and dry the sweating stones.

Nine men and women stood at a distance in a motionless tableau, staring at the beautiful young Lady Anne MacRaeggan, who sat motionless in a high-back intricately carved chair, her glorious red hair shimmering down over the torn and stained bodice of her green velvet gown. She glared back at them, large green eyes filled with hatred, face drained of color, and her lips tightly compressed to hold back the cries of corroding terror that her pride refused to voice. Her eyes fastened on the tall, imposing figure of Sir James MacOrvan, Laird of the Clan MacOrvan, whose black hair was touched with silver and who wore the MacOrvan plaid, pleated into kilts and caught at the shoulder by a silver brooch set with a magnificent emerald that flashed myriad lights when touched by a sudden burst of firelight.

"You slaughtered all my clansmen today! *All the MacRaeggans! Why?*" she shrieked in despair, leaning forward. "Our clans weren't friendly, but we never *murdered* each other, here on Mull and Morven! You and my . . . my . . . *father*"—her voice grew tight around the word, as if it choked her—"fought against the English at the Battle of Flodden. And again . . . just *days* ago!"

He stared back at her from a face that seemed to be chiseled from the same unyielding stone as his castle. Only his black-lashed, deep blue eyes were alive with a crazed hypnotic stare as he moved slowly toward her. "My son Richard . . . my beloved son and heir . . . was murdered on that battlefield three days ago . . . *by another Scotsman . . . your father!*" he bellowed, without a trace of the usual Scottish burr.

She sat motionless, mouth gaping, eyes wide with horror. "No!" she said in a strangled whisper. "You lie!"

"I don't lie, Lady Anne!" His face was runneled with lines of pain. "Your father accused Richard of cowardice on that battlefield! *Cowardice!* I thought it was the *English* who killed him! That's what I was supposed to think! But it was your cursed father who sent me Richard's head, wrapped in the MacOrvan plaid." His words thinned to a moan and died to a gurgle in his throat. "So your father and all his clansmen deserved to die!" With an effort he controlled his rage, but now the softness of his voice seemed to hold an even greater menace. "Yesterday I was informed of your father's heinous treachery, but we waited until today, when you returned for the holidays, from your fancy school in Inverness. I wanted my revenge *complete!*"

"You devil! You unholy devil!" she shrilled, helplessly clawing at the air as if longing to kill him with her own hands.

A cold smile touched the corners of his lips. "Only your grandmother and your two small brothers escaped, but we'll find them soon enough! Your two brothers will die, but your grandmother"—his tongue traced the outline of his lips as if he were already tasting the sweetness of triumph—"your grandmother, Lady Catherine

MacRaeggan, will live . . . to agonize every hour of every day over *you*, her cherished granddaughter. *You, too, will be allowed to live, Lady Anne . . . but you will pray for death!*" His eyes were alight with a triumphant glitter. "People will turn away from you. Mothers will hide their children's eyes, so they won't look on your face! So what man would want you? You will never marry! Never bear issue!" His voice rose. "That will be the end of the MacRaeggan Clan! *It will be no more!*"

For a long moment Lady Anne stared at him, transfixed in frozen disbelief, then, abruptly, she collapsed back against the chair, gasping and shuddering. When she looked up at him again, her eyes blazed with terrible fury. "*I call a curse down on you, James MacOrvan . . . Laird of the Clan MacOrvan!*" she spat at last in a low, tremulous voice. "*May you know all the tortures of the eternally damned . . . before you . . . strangle to death . . . in your own blood!*"

The sound of many footsteps, echoing heavily along the stone corridor, filled the screaming silence with a sense of impending evil. As one, all heads swiveled toward the door. Sir James MacOrvan turned to look at the beautiful young girl. She was now carved from the marble of abject terror, her eyes riveted on the doorway, her ear tuned to the next footsteps. . . .

The storm had passed and a full moon frosted a glitter of diamonds over the new crust of snow and pasted the towers and turrets of Castle Gullhaven—the ancient stronghold of the Clan MacRaeggan—like a black silhouette against the whitened bens. The two MacOrvan clansmen deposited the limp form of Lady Anne unceremoniously on the floor of the Great Hall and then joined their two companions in the keep of the silent castle. Many eyes watched as they hid themselves in the trees near the castle to wait for Lady Catherine and the two small boys to come to the rescue of Lady Anne. But they were sightless eyes of the dead of the Clan MacRaeggan.

The minutes seemed like hours to Lady Catherine as she struggled on, putting one foot automatically in front of the other, often sinking through the crust of snow and losing her balance. Sometimes she would lie there for a moment, every nerve and muscle screaming for rest, her mind numb with the unbearable cold and pain. But the thought of the inhuman monster, Sir James MacOrvan, and the sweet revenge they would have one day, if they could only survive, drove her to her feet to stumble after the shadowy figures ahead. She was grateful for the man's heavy clothing she wore, and it no longer bothered her that Duncan MacDonald had stripped it from a slain MacOrvan lying in the courtyard. How fortunate it was that Duncan found us, before the MacOrvans did! she thought fuzzily. Duncan and his man, Seth, had been traveling home from a funeral at Iona when they came upon her two young grandsons, Keith and Roger, who were returning from school for the holidays, unaware of the ghastly battle that had been fought at Gullhaven. No one had met the boys at the boat landing, and Duncan had given them a lift, planning to seek shelter from the storm, himself, at Gullhaven.

They had found Lady Catherine in the Great Hall of the castle, where she had fallen, unconscious, during the fight, into a deep window recess. She must have clutched at the heavy draperies as she fell and they had come down, covering her slight body and hiding her until the MacOrvans wound their way in drunken victory back to their castle fortress. Duncan had hidden them in the secret room, dug out under the tiles of the kitchen floor, where contraband goods or a fugitive clansman had ofttimes been hidden by the MacRaeggan Clan in the past two hundred years, then set out for Castle MacOrvan to learn the fate of Lady Anne, from unsuspecting servants too drunk with the spoils of war to guard their tongues. How they managed it, Lady Catherine wasn't sure. All she knew was that they had discovered and silently *dispatched* some hidden MacOrvan men; had found Lady Anne, unconscious and badly hurt, on the floor of the Great Hall; and were now fleeing with them to find some possible sanctuary. What clan would protect them from the powerful MacOrvans?

Lady Catherine shuddered uncontrollably. It all still seemed like an horrendous nightmare! The MacOrvans had struck Gullhaven

Castle in the middle of a holiday banquet. One minute everyone was laughing and dancing and the next minute had been ghastly bedlam. It had been such a festive banquet, she recalled through a haze of unreality, trying to ignore the pain of every footstep. It was planned as a surprise for Lady Anne on her return from school in Inverness for the Christmas season and to celebrate a most successful battle with the English three days earlier. Anne had been a vision of loveliness in the new green velvet gown. The sleeves were tight at the shoulders, wide and full at the wrists, with wide, turned-back cuffs lined with gold and green brocade. It was tight at her tiny waist, and the skirt opened from there down to reveal an underskirt of the same elegant brocade that lined the sleeves.

The MacRaeggan Clan of the Isles had danced to the shrill skirl of the bagpipes, drinking one another's health in the heady ales and wines before settling down to the groaning banquet tables. In the confusion of music and laughter and the weaving of tall tales, no one heard the stealthy approach of the Clan MacOrvan until their savage war cry split the air. So no one had been prepared. But . . . why should they have been *prepared?* Suddenly Lady Catherine's feet sank through the crust of snow and she just stood there, weaving back and forth, too weary to extricate herself. With a hopeless cry she collapsed, scarcely aware of the ice against her face or the flow of tears freezing on her cheeks. "It wasn't my son who killed Richard MacOrvan," she wept. "He knew nothing about it! Someone lied! But WHO? and WHY? Who could benefit by such a hideous and evil falsehood? Who?"

Still clad in his full tartan dress, Sir James MacOrvan paced up and down his Great Hall, observed only by two mastiffs who hugged the fire and idly thumped their tails against the stone hearth each time he passed. He was half drunk from the long night's wait and muttering ferocious plans for the punishment of the men he had sent on a simple enough errand and who hadn't returned. "Four husky men against one frail grandmother past childbearing age and two brats!" he growled, throwing himself down into a carved highback chair fit for a king and stretching his booted feet to the fire.

He poured himself another drink and took it down in one gulp, scowling as he did so. *Why* hadn't Ronald MacRaeggan been alert for his enemy? If he, James MacOrvan, had killed a laird's son, he would be prepared to do battle anytime, anyplace! They didn't even have their weapons at hand! He shook his head, fuzzily trying to figure out the oddity of the situation that stuck in his craw.

But Ronald MacRaeggan was guilty as hell! His own two clansmen had revealed it. The two Ewan brothers, distant relatives from a sept of the MacRaeggan Clan, had witnessed it with their own eyes. They had come to him, right here at Castle MacOrvan, and willingly signed a paper stating they had witnessed the murder and heard the instructions of Ronald MacRaeggan to send the head to Sir James MacOrvan, who was away in the Highlands when the battle between the Scots and English took place. And what did it matter that he had promised the Ewan brothers sanctuary; promised them the MacRaeggan lands and Castle Gullhaven, as payment for their information? They were scum of the earth, bearing tales against their own laird, no matter how they hated him. And now, in proper payment for their treachery, the Ewan brothers were no more. Good riddance! Clan justice and clan revenge, although not condoned publicly, were understood privately!

He shifted heavily in his chair, staring into the fire. There would be a great hue and cry over it all. Lady Catherine's brother, Lord Birchmont, of London, would lodge a formal complaint against him with his English King Henry VIII, who in turn would petition strongly to King James V, of Scotland, to bring him to trial and . . . execution. He gave a derisive bark of laughter. James V was only a small boy and Scotland was being governed by regents, now that his widowed mother, Queen Margaret, had married the Red Douglas, Earl of Angus, and had forfeited her authority as regent or tutrix of the infant king. The present governor, the Duke of Albany, had been brought from France, so his allegiance was to France, not England. He spoke only French; he was next in line for the throne of Scotland, should anything happen to the small James V, and he didn't care for King Henry VIII. King Henry, it seemed, didn't like or trust the duke, so both were unlikely to honor each other's requests. Thus it would seem that the law at this time in Scotland had no teeth! Oh, a complaint would be filed with the Privy Council, but it would come to nothing because, he, James Mac-Orvan, would be ready for them with ample proof that he was justified in his revenge against the MacRaeggans . . . and he had it in writing! He smiled in grim satisfaction at his own cleverness. Abruptly he scowled again, and smashed his tankard on the table.

"Thomas!" he bellowed.

A bent wisp of a man scurried out of the shadows and stood nervously shifting from one foot to another, alert to duck if something were thrown at him. "Aye, m'lud?"

"Rouse up ten of the men. Put some food on the table, and be quick about it! We leave in the hour for Castle Gullhaven. We'll find out what happened to that scurvy four I sent . . . and we'll bring back the heads of the two MacRaeggan whelps and write 'finis' to that cursed MacRaeggan Clan *forever!*"

Lady Anne lay on a mound of sheepskins piled on the dirt floor near the smoky peat fire. The crofter's cottage of stones chinked with mud was surprisingly clean; even the rushes that covered the floor smelled fresh, instead of sour and vermin-ridden, as was often the case. She still hadn't really opened her eyes, nor had she spoken, but her tormented cries had diminished since the hot broth, mixed with a concoction of poppy juice and chamomile and a bit of dried leaves of the mint that grew along the streams in the summer, had been forced between her lips. Lady Catherine had gently massaged her throat to make her swallow, and at least she'd kept it down.

Duncan squatted by the older woman. "Lady Catherine," he began in an urgent whisper, "we must make plans . . ."

She looked up at him without answering, irrelevantly noting the tired lines etched into his young face.

"We can't travel much farther with Lady Anne."

She drew in a sharp breath. "What do you mean? We can't leave her here! James MacOrvan will follow us like a bloodhound! Whom can we trust to give her shelter and care?" Her face suddenly lighted up. "Duncan . . . the nuns! We can trust the nuns!"

For the first time he smiled. "Of course! But not here in Scotland.

We'll have to get her to the nearest place in England. York! We must get her to York; then I can take you and your grandsons to your brother, Lord Birchmont, in London." He cast a warning glance at the crofter and his wife, a little distance away, watching them covertly as they kept their hands busy at small tasks, and lowered his voice even further. "If we can get to the village, I have a friend with a large boat who can take us through the Sound of Mull . . . to Oban . . . and from there to Edinburgh and down to York. Are you up to it, Lady Catherine?" He glanced at her sharply.

She looked around at her three sleeping grandchildren and felt a stab of excruciating pain. They were all that was left of the noble MacRaeggan Clan . . . God help them all! "Yes! Yes, I'll make it!" she assured Duncan grimly. "We'll *all* make it!"

It took days of unbelievably difficult travel before they neared the bustling City of York, capital of the North Country and second city of the realm, situated at the junction of the Ouse and Foss rivers, and site of the first Roman fortification, called Eboracum, in AD 71.

"We'd best separate and meet outside St. Clements nunnery," Duncan said, reaching over to catch the reins of Lady Catherine's horse and hold it close to his own so they could talk. Her granddaughter had now been put astride the horse, like a man, behind Duncan, tied with a rope to his waist and with her cheek against his back. She had periods of feverish consciousness but, thanks be to God, she didn't seem to be aware of her surroundings or the bandages on her head and chest. "I'll enter York first, with Lady Anne and Keith. Seth"—he turned to his grizzled manservant—"you wait an hour, then come in with your wife"—he nodded toward Lady Catherine, who was now dressed in a rough skirt and cloak—"and your young son." He indicated little Roger, who was having trouble keeping his horse in check.

She nodded wearily. "It just *might* throw the MacOrvans off the track."

"Just might," he agreed without too much conviction. As he was leaving, he suddenly turned back to her. "Why St. Clements nunnery? Wouldn't you be better to take her to St. Mary's Abbey?

They are known for their hospitality, especially to someone of title . . ."

"I know, Duncan. That's precisely why I chose St. Clements. As head of the largest and wealthiest Benedictine monastery in the North of England, the Abbot of St. Mary's must entertain all the noble and important visitors to York. It would be almost impossible to keep Lady Anne's presence a secret."

"Yes, I see," he said finally, then he raised his hand in good-bye and was off with his ill-assorted party.

It was late morning when an exhausted, mud-stained Lady Catherine and her two companions entered York from the north, crossing what remained of the fourteenth-century drawbridge and passing through the battlemented city walls by way of Bootham Bar, one of the four medieval gateways, with its narrow slit windows, its ancient portcullis and castellated turrets. The cobblestone streets, slick with melting snow, made uneasy footing for the horses, and Lady Catherine could hear Seth cursing softly under his breath. For the first time in a long time she felt a little more secure. The nuns and the monks were often more skilled in medicine than many of the physicians, and she would trust them to heal her granddaughter's battered mind as well as her body.

She lifted her eyes to the majesty of York Minster, riding high above the patchwork of red-tiled roofs and denuded trees, and recalled fleetingly how overwhelmed she had been on her first visit to that magnificent cathedral with its treasury of stained glass, breathtaking arches, and columns of Purbeck marble. It had been on the occasion of her trip from London to Edinburgh for her marriage into the MacRaeggan Clan. How ironic it was, she thought bitterly, to see everything unchanged when her own life and that of her family was destroyed or shattered beyond mending. "Let us find sanctuary here, please God," she murmured, urging her tired mount on through the narrow, winding streets and past the line of shops in Newgate Market she'd once thought so intriguing.

The Reverend Mother put the chamois pouch of money on the table and glanced sharply at the woman who had just given it to her. In spite of her rough garments she was obviously a lady, some-one of importance and someone in grave trouble, she reasoned, not letting her thoughts disturb the tranquillity of her expression. And of course it concerned the beautiful young girl, now being attended by Sisters Emily and Theresa, who had been so brutally hurt. But why was it necessary to be so secretive? As one of their faith, she must know the sisters would never violate a confidence.

"Is it enough?" Lady Catherine began anxiously.

"Very generous." The Reverend Mother leaned forward to look into her visitor's face. "But, my dear lady, payment is not necessary. We welcome anyone in need."

"I know, of course. But you may have to keep my grand"—she broke off, aware she had made an irreversible slip, then continued with a sigh—"my . . . granddaughter . . . for some time, until she is able to travel."

The Abbess nodded several times, closing and opening her eyes thoughtfully. So it was her granddaughter. She might have guessed, although there was little or no resemblance between that red-haired beauty and this silver-haired, gently bred woman with the saddest brown eyes she'd ever seen. "Where can I reach you when she has recovered?"

"I'll get in touch with you, Reverend Mother. Oh . . ." She reached over and covered the Abbess' hand with hers. "It isn't that I don't trust you. I'm entrusting you with the most precious person left to me! But for your own protection—and the protection of my granddaughter, who must be kept hidden—the less you know, the better." Seeing no change of expression on the Abbess' face, she shrugged helplessly. "All I feel I can tell you is that this concerns a very powerful and ruthless man who will stop at nothing to carry out his evil and mistaken revenge. If you don't know to whom you are giving shelter you can't be blamed . . . or harmed."

"We are under God's protection," the Reverend Mother reminded her gently.

"I know. I know, but I must insist on sparing you any needless . . . trouble." She stood up, slight form erect, unmistakably the aris-tocrat in spite of the rough peasant dress. "We must be on our way,

Reverend Mother. My deepest thanks for your kindness and the hospitality of St. Clements this past night. May God bless you for your understanding heart . . ." Tears brimmed her eyes and threatened to fall, and she turned quickly away.

The Abbess got to her feet and put her hands on her shoulders to turn her gently to face her. "Don't worry, my child. Your granddaughter will be nursed back to health. Remember, she is under God's wing . . . and may He watch over you and carry you safely to your destination."

"Thank you, Reverend Mother." Lady Catherine was weeping openly now. "My . . . my granddaughter's name is . . . Anne . . ." She embraced the kindly woman, then hurried out into the courtyard, where Duncan held the steaming horses, which were stamping their feet against the cold. Her two sober grandsons and a silent Seth were already mounted. Duncan gave her a leg up and they were off, riding fast into the gray winter's dawn, heading for London.

The Abbess watched from the window of her study until they were swallowed up by the heavy mist. She shook her head time and again as she sat down at the refectory table that served as her desk. This entire situation made her uneasy. It had so many dark and ugly overtones, she couldn't seem to rid herself of the feeling that there were terrible trials ahead . . . for everyone. She shook her head again, mentally chiding herself for her unworthy, negative thoughts. I will pray about it at Vespers this afternoon, she promised.

September

Her feet had been bathed, the viaticum ministered, the homily of death had been read. The priest straightened up, and for a long moment he and the Reverend Mother stood looking down at the girl in the narrow bed. Her eyes were closed, her face waxen; only the brilliant red hair spread over the pillow seemed to be alive. The Abbess sighed deeply. "Call me if you need me, Sister Emily."

"I will, Reverend Mother, thank you." Sister Emily watched the priest and the head of the nunnery as they crossed the narrow cell and went out the door, closing it softly behind them, then she wrang out the cloth again in cool water and continued to bathe the perspiration from Anne's face and neck.

"You're doing fine, dear child," she soothed, patting the delicate hands that were gripping the cover so tightly she couldn't pry them loose. "It won't be long now." Her heart ached with love for this dear child who had wormed her way into all their hearts these past months. She was so sweet, so gentle, so tractable as she moved through the nunnery like a pale, fragile ghost, a being from another world. It had taken some three months for her to gain enough strength to be up and around, and she was well into her fifth month of pregnancy before any of the sisters realized she was changing shape.

When the Reverend Mother talked to her about the coming event, Anne had smiled sweetly and clapped her hands happily like a child. Yes, a child. That's what she had become. Whatever dark and brutal tragedy had befallen her, it was locked forever behind the innermost doors of her childlike mind. And now she was giving her last breath, the last ounce of her pitiful strength, to bring into the world the tiny creature within her. Sister Emily choked back the tears of love and pity and prayed to God for strength to help ease the suffering of this beautiful lost child.

Anne's agonized screams pierced Sister Emily through the heart. "Take deep breaths. Breathe deeply, Anne, and when the pain strikes, push. Push. Grab my hands and push hard!"

"I'm . . . trying . . ." Anne gasped faintly. "I'm . . . trying!" Then she screamed again and again, digging her nails into the sister's hands.

Some time later Sister Emily placed a swaddled bundle within the curve of the young mother's arm. "Anne, it's a girl, a beautiful, healthy girl with black silky hair." When there was no response, she shook her gently. "Anne . . . look at your lovely daughter."

Anne slowly opened her eyes, already glazed over with death, and laboriously turned her head to look at the sleeping baby. She tried to move her hand to touch the tiny pink fist, but hadn't the strength.

"My . . . baby . . ." she breathed with a sigh. "She's . . . beauti·

ful." A smile touched her lips, then she frowned slightly, as if trying to remember something that kept escaping her. "Sister Emily . . ."

"Yes, my dear . . ."

"Name . . . her . . . Catherine, please. I . . . somehow . . . love . . . Catherine."

"Very well, dear. We'll name her Catherine."

"Thank you . . . dear . . . Sister . . ." Her head dropped heavily to the side and she was still.

Sister Emily's tears flowed freely now, running down her wrinkled cheeks and dropping on the little Catherine's head as if baptizing her with a special blessing.

CHAPTER TWO

CATHERINE . . . 1533

Catherine stood on a hill overlooking the Yorkshire moors that stretched in undulating greens and purples as far as the eye could see. The teasing breeze lifted silken tendrils of her long black hair, tugging them loose from the demure cap that was part of her homespun daily dress. She pulled the cap off and sent it flying.

"Spring is here! It's spring!" she called out, setting free the joy that had become too explosive to be contained within her slender sixteen-year-old body. She ran down the hill and over the moors, holding her skirts high to avoid catching them on the heather or scrubby oak. If she came back with a tear in her skirt, Reverend Mother would shake her head and remind her, in a tone of determined patience, that she was no longer a child, that she was almost a woman and must start to act like one.

Catherine would listen, head bent in short-lived penitence, then she'd raise her head and look at the Abbess, her green eyes shining. "But it's so beautiful, Reverend Mother. The breeze is warm and fragrant . . . the ling on the moors is so green . . . the heather so many shades of purple . . . and there's the sound of the bees—"

"I'm quite aware of the beauty of the moors in the spring," she broke in coolly, "but there's beauty all around us, if we can but *see* it! However, it must not deter us from our appointed tasks!" And she would send Catherine off to weed the vegetable garden with Sister Emily. Catherine didn't see the look of love in the Reverend Mother's eyes as she watched the lovely young woman's graceful exit, nor did she hear the helpless sigh or the soft entreaty to God to give her proper guidance.

For days thereafter, Catherine would be the paragon of industry, working in the gardens with her beloved Sister Emily, mending the nuns' robes with skillful stitches, standing by the hour in the washhouse, soaked with perspiration as she ironed the nuns' stiff white wimples; then practicing on the harpsichord and small organ and earning Sister Theresa's praise for her perfection in Latin, French, and mathematics. Then, inevitably, she would break loose again and roam the moors for a long glorious day before returning to do the waiting penance.

She stretched out on the ground on her back in the thick cotton grass and looked up at the sky. It was swept clean of clouds, and how blue-blue it was! Had an artist ever been able to capture that intense color and still make it look realistic? She lazily turned her head to look at the moors, beautiful in their soft spring dress of purple heather, the white blossoms of the ling interspersed with great clumps of yellow gorse. Here and there in the hollows and folds of the hills, where rain was caught and held longer, she glimpsed the shiny yellow of crowsfoot and the waxy white of marsh marigolds, along with their pale yellow cousins. A lark's song mixed sweetly with the hum of the bees, and high above, a hawk was pinned to the sky in suspended motion. There mountain linnets swooped low over the furzes to draw attention of the hawks away from their nests. Late in the summer the ling would be burned to an autumnal brown, the heather would dry out, and the moors would again stretch remote and treeless, covered with an ugly scree that offended the eye and trapped the feet of an occasional traveler.

A solitary puffy white cloud floated slowly across her vision, heralding the return of its puffy white companions. The fresh breeze molded the cloud into a plump chicken, then pulled it into one of those strange elephants with a long exploring trunk. Catherine laughed aloud and for a few minutes happily imagined the shapes of birds, animals, and people. Ah, there was an outline of the Reverend Mother, with the white stiff wimple surrounding her proper face. It had been a very sober face of late, and Catherine felt sure it had to do with the action of King Henry's cruel destruction of some of the monasteries, their treasures carted away to swell the king's coffers and the monks often turned out to beg or starve. If anyone openly voiced his objections to the king's cold-blooded acts, he was hauled off to face trial and, more often than not, the chopping block.

Catherine had seen an example of that only a few days ago, when she was on an errand for the Abbess. Two men, a little worse for the ale they'd drunk, were hotly arguing the situation in front of a tavern where a small crowd had gathered. The older man furiously defended the actions of the king, declaring that the Catholic churches owned too much property, were too rich, too powerful, and too uncaring of the needs of the common man. The younger man, his red hair as fiery as his words, shouted that he'd had a bellyful of King Henry's laws. His family was overtaxed, underfed, and he couldn't get enough steady work to keep a decent roof over their heads.

"All the king cared about was breaking away from the Pope and the Church of Rome! And now he has had himself declared the Supreme Head of the English Church!" the young redhead bellowed, in the perfect English of a scholar. "And why? All because he wanted a divorce from Catherine of Aragon, so he could marry Anne Boleyn, and the Pope refused." The crowd "oooohhhhed" and "aaahed" at his boldness, but the young man took no notice. "And now that he had rid himself of Catherine and married Anne, what was the king doing? He was tearing down the monasteries and disposing of their wealth and lands as he pleased! But what about those men who worked those lands? Where could they find work to feed their families? Where?" His angry words were still sizzling in the air when three men in the king's uniform dragged him away. He had committed high treason, and he would be killed for sure, Catherine thought, with the bitter taste of gall in her mouth and a heavy sadness in her heart.

She had mentioned it to Sister Emily as they bent to their weeding. The nun wouldn't discuss the right or wrong of it, but she had sat back on her heels, supple even in these late years, and said:

"What good did the young man accomplish? He will die for voicing his opinions, and what of the family he leaves behind? The young wife will die early of hard work, trying to feed her small children. Or, in these difficult times, she might steal to keep body and soul together and end up in prison, or on the stocks. If she's one of the fortunate ones, perhaps she'll have a chance to take a second husband . . . an older man . . . to care for her family—" She broke off abruptly, as if afraid she had said too much, gone too far and too out of her role of a nun, who enjoyed special privileges as a teacher and sometimes companion to this young charge of St. Clements.

Catherine scowled suddenly. There, in cloud picture, was the form of Lord Feldstone, even to the shape of his loathsome big belly. She couldn't see his little beady eyes, but with a shudder her mind's eye remembered them. He had ridden over to St. Clements some two weeks ago with his scrawny, haughty wife. They said they had heard of Catherine, a young lady who would seem well fitted to the role of governess to their two lumbering children. Catherine didn't mention that she had seen Lord Feldstone ogling her several times and had heard him making inquiries as to her name and residence. Inexperienced as she was with regard to a man-woman relationship, she felt immediately endangered in this man's presence. He reminded her of a fat rat she had cornered in the stillroom, the way his nose twitched and his lips lifted in a semblance of a smile to show large yellowing teeth.

The Abbess had agreed, with some reluctance, that Catherine would go to them at the summer's end, when most of the preserving of vegetables and fruits would be done and she could better do without her help.

"I have no choice, my dear," the Abbess said later. "You will be seventeen in September. You are almost a grown woman. You have never chosen to become a member of the order and," she sighed, "perhaps rightly so. It takes great dedication . . . control . . . selflessness . . . and you are like quicksilver . . . never still. You want to reach out and embrace the world and explore its every corner . . ." She smiled her understanding and sighed again as she looked at her hands, clasped in front of her on the desk. Then she looked up intently into the face of the girl they'd all come to love. "I was so hoping we would have news of your family, my child. Your great-grandmother, who was a lady, had a great love for your mother. She left money for her care and promised to keep in. touch with us. But, as you know, we have never heard more. Some disaster must have befallen her."

"I'll work hard, Reverend Mother. Even harder," Catherine said in desperation. "I promise I won't give you further trouble. I'll not run to the moors . . ."

The Abbess stood up and came around to stand by her charge, putting her hands on her shoulders and regarding her with the deepest compassion. "My dear, the decision has nothing to do with your days on the moors. I understand the need, the excitement, the response to beauty within you, but we can no longer keep you here. It's time you left St. Clements. We have equipped you with a good education, even superior to that of many young ladies of the court, so you can make your way in the outside world."

"But . . . Lord Feldstone . . ." Catherine began.

"Lord Feldstone holds an important position in the City of York, and in these trying days we need every possible friend." The Abbess sat down again at her desk. "They will treat you well, Catherine. I have their promise." She moved things around on the desk several times, the usual indication that she was wrestling with a heavy problem. It was some time before she looked up again at the young girl, and then it was with a startled expression, as if she hadn't remembered her presence.

"Oh, you may go, Catherine. Tell Sister Grace to provide you with some cloth from the storeroom, so you may make yourself two new dresses, one for every day and one for better wear. You'll need them in your new position."

Catherine said no more, but she decided she'd never go to Lord Feldstone's. She'd run away—maybe to London—and find work. She hated the thought of hurting the Reverend Mother, but she hated the thought of Lord Feldstone much more.

Catherine closed her eyes. The sun was warm and soothing on her eyelids. She felt as if she were floating on top of the fat white clouds, pulled willy-nilly by the breeze. When she awoke, the sun was high in the west. "Ooooooh! I'll catch it this time. It must be almost the supper hour!" She jumped up and ran, startling a rabbit, who darted back into his hole, which was cleverly camouflaged by a swirl of heavy bracken. Her foot caught in a patch of scree and she tumbled headlong into a mound of heather. As she got to her feet and was brushing herself off, her eye was caught by a cluster of rare white bell heather almost hidden by its purple cousin.

"Oh, how beautiful," she crooned, quickly gathering a bouquet to take back to the Abbess. It may not soften her disapproval but it would bring her great pleasure. She buried her face in the herblike fragrance. The white heather was said to bring a person good fortune! She broke off a piece and tucked it into her bodice. That would go under her pillow tonight. On second thought, she tucked in a second piece. She knew Sister Emily didn't hold with such silliness, but she'd slip into her little narrow cell of a room and put it under her pillow, anyway, because of all the sisters she loved her the best and wanted her remaining years to be tranquil and happy.

As she neared St. Clements, Catherine stopped for a moment, looking up at the gray stone buildings with their delicately carved arches and high windows painted gold by the sun. It's strange, she thought as her eyes drank in the beauty of the old nunnery, how you don't appreciate something until you realize you're going to lose it. This is my home . . . the only home I've ever known . . . and I'll have to leave it at summer's end. She impatiently blinked away her tears and ran on, trying, unsuccessfully, to outrace her gnawing fears.

Sister Emily was hovering inside the high back gate and she waddled forward, clasping and unclasping her hands as Catherine let herself in.

"Oh, thank goodness, child! I thought you'd never get here!" She cast a knowing glance at her torn skirt. "I don't need to ask where you've been! Oh . . . bell heather! How lovely!" She clapped her hands, momentarily forgetting her agitation. "Oh, but, Catherine . . . you must hurry and make yourself presentable. The Reverend Mother is waiting for you!"

"I'm sure she is!" she said with a sigh as she hurried along at Sister Emily's side, past the flourishing vegetable garden, the herb garden, and the lovely rose garden heady with fragrant, colorful bloom and in through the kitchen way, where silent sisters were finishing the preparation of the evening meal.

"Oh, it's different this time," Sister Emily puffed as her short legs tried to keep pace. "There's a visitor to see you. He's been here some two and a half hours!"

"A *visitor*? To see *me*?" She stopped so abruptly, Sister Emily ran right into her, and for a moment they laughingly steadied each other. Catherine looked down into the shriveled-apple face of the little nun, whose dark eyes were popping with curiosity. "Who is it, Sister Emily? Who . . . ?" Her shoulders suddenly sagged. "Oh. Lord Feldstone!"

"No. No, Catherine. It's a stranger, very handsomely dressed. The Reverend Mother didn't give his name . . . or where he came from. She just said to send you to her as soon as you returned." Her disappointment was so obvious, Catherine almost laughed aloud.

"I'll tell you about it later," she promised. The little nun tried to act as if it really didn't matter, but the way she happily bustled off, humming a little tune under her breath, ever so softly so as not to disturb the meditation of her sisters, gave away her pleasure.

In her bare little room, Catherine hurriedly poured some cold water in the basin and splashed her hands and face and brushed her hair until all the bits of twigs and leaves were out and the curly mass was shining like black satin. All the time she tidied herself she was wondering if she had committed some terrible crime and this was someone who had come to drag her off to prison. She had only listened to the two men arguing the other day, she hadn't taken part or expressed her views in any way. Or . . . maybe, she thought with a sudden rise in her spirits, it was someone else who had children and wanted a governess. After all, Lord Feldstone wasn't the only wealthy man in York! Or perhaps—the hairbrush hung suspended in midair and her heartbeat quickened painfully—perhaps it was someone from her family. No! She brushed with such vigor, the sharp bristles brought tears to her eyes. No, she didn't dare think along that line. It was too much to hope for and she had been disappointed too many times, hoping and dreaming in vain and looking with anxious eyes at each occasional stranger.

She started out the door, but went back and stripped off her torn homespun dress. The Reverend Mother wouldn't like it if she appeared in front of an important stranger in a torn skirt. She took down the twin of the one she'd been wearing, except this dress had a white lawn partlet that filled in the open neckline.

"Oh, fiddlesticks!" she groaned. The skirt of this dress also had a tear in it. She had meant to mend it today but, instead, she'd gone running out on the moors. She stared at the two new gowns she had finished just yesterday. Did she dare wear the new best one? On sudden impulse she took it down off the line of four wall pegs that served as a clothespress and slid it over her head. The soft mustard-yellow material felt luxurious to her skin, which had known only the scratch of brown homespun, summer and winter, for as long as she could remember. She had painstakingly copied the style from those she had noticed on the fine ladies in the city, and her dress had a square neckline, edged with a bit of black braid that Sister Grace had dug up from heaven knew where in the storeroom. Above the braid ran an inch or two of white linen which Catherine had carefully finished in tiny vertical pleats. The sleeves were puffed at the shoulders, the bodice was tight to the waist, above a full skirt, and she had fastened the dress at the waistline with two hooks hidden underneath.

Reluctantly she put on the white linen cap, pushing it to the back of her head. It had a horseshoe shape to the front, lappets that hung down either side and were split to fit over the front and back of the shoulders. How she hated hats, and hoods, *anything* that made her feel closed in, and finally, rebelliously, she tied the lappets up over the top of her cap so her shiny black hair fell free down her back.

The look of shock on the Reverend Mother's face brought Catherine to an immediate halt. Maybe she'd been too bold, letting her hair hang free under the demure cap. Maybe she didn't like her dress. She had no mirror, so she had only assumed she looked fine. Perhaps she looked frightful!

The gentleman rose from the bench and came toward her. His back was to the window, so momentarily his face was in shadow, but she could see his clothes were like those of the noble gentlemen she'd seen in York. His shoes were of soft cream-colored leather, square-toed and slashed in a pattern to show a rich brocade underneath. His stockings were of a fine plum material and his white linen shirt was handsomely embroidered in black and gold, as was his stomacher and plum velvet doublet, belted at the waist and pleated. As he turned to the Abbess, she saw his short hair was dark brown, lightly peppered with gray, as was the beard that edged his jawline and the moustache above the curve of his lips.

"Reverend Mother?" he urged rather sharply.

"Yes. Yes," she hastened to say, composing herself quickly. "Catherine"—she put out a hand and drew the girl close to her side —"this is Lord John Birchmont, Earl of Birchmont, a relative of yours, who has come from London to inquire for you. He is the nephew of your late great-grandmother, Lady Catherine MacRaeggan."

Catherine was so stunned, she could only gape at him, her eyes wide with shock. Then everything in the room seemed to spin around crazily and her heart hammered so hard she was afraid he could hear it. "Lord . . . Birchmont . . ." she quavered at last, forcing her shaking limbs into an awkward curtsy.

He took her hand and raised her up to face him. He was only her height, which was tall for a girl, so their eyes met on a common level. It was a nice face, she decided foggily. Not really handsome. His high-bridged nose was a little too large, his face too round and fleshy, but his eyes were brown and warm and they told her she was pleasant to look upon.

"How do you do, Catherine?" he said with a smile as he gave her hand a friendly squeeze before dropping it. "To avoid confusion, perhaps you'll address me as 'Uncle John,' and I'll call you 'niece.' You are a niece . . . of sorts . . ." All the time he was talking, he was thinking: Mary will be in a temper, bringing this gorgeous young girl into our home. She's a good woman, Mary, but she won't like the competition for Sheila. Sheila will be jealous of her, but the boys will be her slaves. Aloud he said, "My daughter, Sheila, will welcome a sister of her age and my two small sons, Tom and Jack, will undoubtedly vie for your attention."

The Abbess could see the burgeoning of frantic hope, clouded with disbelief on the face of her young charge. "Please sit down, Lord Birchmont . . . Catherine . . . Perhaps, for Catherine's benefit, you'd be good enough to repeat some of the story you have revealed to me . . . and . . . your plans?"

"Of course, Reverend Mother. I'm sure this must be something of a . . . surprise . . . even a shock . . . to Catherine, after all these years! Your name is Catherine . . . MacRaeggan . . ." He leaned forward, holding her eyes with his as he told her of the slaughter of her clansmen and the escape of the four MacRaeggans. "When your great-grandmother, Lady Catherine, finally arrived at the home of my father, Lord Birchmont, her mind was completely gone. She remembered nothing. Her grandsons, Keith and Roger, told of the bravery of Duncan MacDonald and his man, Seth, who had lost their lives defending them against the attack of footpads outside London. The boys said their sister, Lady Anne, had died at St. Clements and had been left there for burial by the nuns. They'd obviously been told this by their grandmother to protect Lady Anne's whereabouts, in the event she and the boys would be captured before reaching London. So my father had no way of knowing that your mother, Lady Anne, was alive."

He shifted uncomfortably under the steady regard of her large still eyes. "They had the best of care, Catherine," he assured her hastily, "but London was rife with the pox and the plague at that time, and little Roger died . . . and then . . . Lady Catherine. Only Keith lived." He shifted again. "After the death of my father, some fourteen months ago, I found some rambling notes written by Lady Catherine. She had mentioned the name Anne over and over again, along with St. Clements. The more I read the notes, the more convinced I became that I might find Lady Anne alive. Yesterday I came to York on some business for the king and decided to visit St. Clements." He reached over and took her cold hand in his. "I found you, Catherine, and now I'm going to take you home with me. I trust this is to your liking?"

She tried to speak, but the lump in her throat held back the words, so she could only stare from him to the Reverend Mother, unable to make out their features through the mist before her eyes.

"Well, Catherine?" the Abbess urged.

"Oh yes! Yes! Thank you, sir! It's just that . . . that . . . finding a *family* and a new home—all at once—is a little . . . overwhelming!" She got up and made a curtsy, blinking her eyes hard. "I'll be a good, a proper niece, sir! You'll find me a great help."

"I'm sure, my dear," he mumbled, unused to such emotional scenes.

"Catherine is a fine scholar," the Abbess broke in. "Very knowledgeable in French, Latin, mathematics, music . . . so you may find her an able tutor for your young sons."

"Splendid! Splendid! They can use some tutoring!"

Catherine didn't hear the rest of whatever he said. She felt like dancing and running wild and shouting. She had a family! A *family!* She would never have to work for that loathsome Lord Feldstone . . . never have to run away! A sobering thought struck her: How did she have the name MacRaeggan when that was the name of her mother's family? "My . . . *father?*" she inquired softly, looking at her newly found relative. "Was he killed with the MacRaeggans? Would you tell me about my father?" The silence in the room became so absolute it suddenly seemed to surround and stifle her.

"Your . . . father?" he said. "No, no, I can't tell you anything about your father! I'm afraid that's a secret that died with your mother, my dear." He took a deep breath. "We think she might have been secretly married, perhaps to someone her family disapproved of, maybe one of her distant cousins who was there at the festivities and was killed with the rest of the MacRaeggans." The lies came surprisingly easy to his lips. She was now part of his family—a part of the Birchmont bloodline—and he would protect this lovely Catherine with his life, as he would any other of his children. All he could do was give her a happy home as long as possible, and if she found out? Well, he thought with an inward sigh, I'll have to cross that bridge when I come to it!

"Oh." The disappointment of her years of waiting and dreaming was in the single word.

He couldn't trust himself to look into her face for the moment. "There's another matter, a very serious one, which must be discussed now and then buried forever!"

"Yes, sir?"

"You are *never* to use the MacRaeggan name, never admit you are a member of the MacRaeggan Clan! Your name, from this day forward, is Catherine Birchmont! *Birchmont!* And will be Birchmont until you . . . may . . . may choose to change it one day . . . by . . . by marriage."

Her eyes grew enormous. "But why, sir?" she whispered. "Am I not worthy?"

"Of course you're *worthy!*" he snapped, venting his helplessness in anger. His expression softened as he regarded the white distressed face. "It could mean your life or death!" He took her hands in his again and could feel them trembling. "If James MacOrvan knew of your existence—or the existence of your Uncle Keith—it would be signing a death warrant for you both."

Her great green eyes searched his face as if looking for a sign of deception. "Then, my Uncle Keith also has the Birchmont name?"

"Yes," he replied, relieved she was not given to hysterical questions or the vapors, as were some young women he knew. "Shortly after your great-grandmother and her two grandsons arrived at my father's house in London, my own younger brother died of the pox, along with his wife and two sons. His only daughter was staying with an aunt in the country, but she, too, later died of the pox. To protect your two uncles, everyone was made to believe they were my brother's sons, and had not perished, so they safely assumed the Birchmont name. You will assume the name of his daughter. Your Uncle Keith is married and has a small daughter of his own. They are in the Indies right now. Keith is looking after some sugar plantations we have, but they should return before Christmas."

"I see . . ." she said slowly, as the color returned to her face. "Birchmont . . ." Her eyes were thoughtful. "It's for my protection . . ."

"Yes . . . In *every way!*"

"Then it shall be as you wish, and I thank you for your concern!"

She smiled and made a curtsy, this time one worthy of the names of MacRaeggan and Birchmont.

The moon was still riding high when she got out of bed and hurriedly dressed in her old homespun then crept barefooted down the stone stairs and let herself out by way of the kitchen door and into the silver-washed night. The cold air shocked her into complete wakefulness as she moved swiftly down the brick path, past the herb garden, sharp with the smell of thyme and rosemary, past the vegetable garden and then the rose garden, its headiness muted to a delicate fragrance by the night's chill. She unfastened the gate and slid through, fastening it behind her, careful to hold onto the bell that could announce her presence. Then she picked up her skirts and ran, hair streaming behind her as she leaped over the low dry-stone wall and raced across the fields—following the line of irrigation ditches—then headed toward a distant hill massed with dark clumped trees.

The low, rusty iron fence was scarcely distinguishable, but the headstones and crosses that leaned toward each other, as if caught in friendly conversation, gleamed with a false pristine whiteness in the moonlight. Catherine skirted the fence and sank down on a small outcropping of rock that formed a rough bench. Near her feet, sheltered by a hovering tree, was a wooden cross, freshly whitewashed, and at its base a pot of roses and fluffy white chervil that Catherine had placed there this morning on her way to the moors.

This morning! Was it only this morning that I placed those flowers on my mother's grave? Catherine thought. How dramatically my life has changed in a few short hours! As she stared at the cross, her throat tightened with familiar emotion. She'd always rather resented the position of her mother's grave, outside St. Clements cemetery. It was as if she were beyond the pale, not worthy of recognition, as if she would somehow contaminate those enclosed by the protective fence. The Abbess had denied it emphatically, even Sister Emily had assured it wasn't so. Her mother just hadn't been "of" the order at St. Clements. Catherine sighed heavily. At least they hadn't buried her in the village cemetery without a marker, but she'd often wondered if they'd known her mother's noble name and if she had been properly married . . . would they have buried her within the privileged fence? The cross that marked her grave had finally rotted at the base, and Sister Emily had helped Catherine to patch it and drive it down again into the ground with a heavy rock, but the name of "Anne" had long ago been worn away.

"Lady Anne MacRaeggan!" Catherine murmured, relishing the sound of the lovely name rolling off her tongue. "Mother . . . my mother . . . Lady Anne MacRaeggan! I'm a MacRaeggan! A MacRaeggan!" She was suddenly filled with a deep sense of pride and a niggling reluctance that she'd have to use the Birchmont name. But only for the time being! Only until I know all the facts! she decided fiercely. For to deny the MacRaeggan name forever is to deny my own mother, and that I'll *never* do! Her thoughts turned to Sir James MacOrvan, Laird of the Clan MacOrvan, who had ordered the senseless slaughter of the MacRaeggan Clan. How could anyone be that wicked . . . that bloodthirsty? And why was he still alive . . . still free to enjoy life, to act the king? Men lived or died at his whim as he commanded and dismissed! A rage unlike anything she'd ever experienced welled up from deep within her and shook her with its intensity. He had slaughtered almost her entire family; only she and her Uncle Keith survived! Somehow, someday, she would see that he paid for his heinous crimes! How she could effect this she didn't know, but she knew, with a sense of unshakable confidence, that she could, and *would!*

She ducked instinctively as something swooshed by her head and landed in the tree overhead, followed immediately by a soft garbling and an answering "t-hoot! t-hoot!" She smiled as she looked up. The mother owl was back from her hunting trip and feeding her two little owlets. She stood up, reluctant to leave, knowing that this might well be the last time she'd come this way. She had sat here many times before, not in sadness but just with the need to feel closer to the mother she knew only through Sister Emily's description of her sweetness, her gentleness, and her beauty. Now she didn't know how to say good-bye. She gave herself a mental shake.

"Only her earthly remains are here, silly girl!" she chided herself in a whisper. "Her spirit is still with you, and always will be!" Nevertheless, as she walked away, she stopped and turned to look back. A passing cloud obscured the moon, plunging the cemetery in stygian darkness. Then, as she strained to see, a bit of the moon peeked through, pinpointing just the cross on her mother's grave with a single beautiful ray of white light. A little cry escaped her lips. It was as if her mother smiled at her for a moment. As she stared, the moon came out again in all its glory, silvering the land, and she was conscious of the cold benumbing her bare feet and of the cut of the night breeze that raised goose bumps along her arms. She started to run, but she stumbled often on her way back to St. Clements, her vision clouded by streaming tears.

The stars dimmed and disappeared finally into the deep gray of the predawn hours; the gray gave grudging way to breathtaking pinks and ripples of gold. By the time the sun tipped the tall spires of York Minster in the distance, she was out of bed, washed, and into the second new gown she'd made, of a lovely deep green material. She packed her few belongings in a small case, remade the hard, narrow cot with fresh coarse linen sheets, and swept the stone floor with a stiff rush broom, then stood looking around for the last time. She closed the door softly behind her and hurried down the stairs and into the dim refectory, where the nuns waited for her, along with the Abbess and Lord Birchmont. She kissed each nun in turn, murmuring her loving thanks, then she was standing in front of Sister Emily. "Oh, Sister Emily! Dear Sister Emily, I'll miss you so! You have truly been like a mother to me!" she cried, enveloping her in her strong young arms and hugging her fiercely. Then she placed her hands gently under her chin, looking down into the wrinkled face. "If you ever need me, Sister Emily, you know where to find me, and I'll come running!"

"Thank you, dear Catherine," the sister said simply, uncaring of the tears rolling down her cheeks and dripping off her stubby nose. "And may God watch over you, and give you guidance and keep you in safety for the rest of your life." She made the sign of the cross, as did those assembled.

Catherine genuflected before the Abbess and held her hand for a moment against her lips before getting to her feet. "I'll be eternally grateful for the love and care you have given me all these years, Reverend Mother, and I thank you from the bottom of my heart!"

The Abbess kissed her on both cheeks. "Go with God, dear child. You have given us much happiness."

They left the nunnery by the back way, avoiding the main roads, circling up and around to the north side of the city, almost as if her uncle were attempting to cover their tracks.

"We meet them there." Lord Birchmont reined in his horse and pointed ahead to the sign of the Blue Swan, suspended over the heavy mullioned windows of a brick and timbered building. Above the name the figure of a blue swan was worked in iron, for the benefit of the many who couldn't read.

Three men stood near the entrance to the tavern. One raised his hand in greeting and the other two touched their caps, so Catherine knew the young, handsome man was William Lester, son of a friend of her uncle's and the other two were a groom and manservant. Her uncle had told her that William had traveled to York with them on business for his father and would accompany them back to London. The larger the party, the safer was the traveling. In this day of vast numbers of men without work, or a way to support themselves and their families, traveling on the road was dangerous. From the large, workless vagrant class, often called the "sturdy beggars," bands of outlaws were formed, and they robbed and killed and terrorized as if it were their right.

"Well, William, did you conclude your business satisfactorily?" Lord Birchmont called, jumping down and clasping his hand.

"Fine. Fine, thank you, sir," he replied, without taking his eyes off the vision on the horse. Then, as the groom held her mount steady, William freed his hand and leaped over to lift her down.

"This is my niece, Catherine Birchmont, daughter of my late brother, Francis. Catherine . . . William Lester, whose father, the Duke of Chatham, is my most esteemed friend." He made the introductions in determined joviality, groaning inwardly. He had never seen William look this way at his daughter, Sheila, and his wife, Mary, was doing everything in her power to arrange her marriage into the wealthy and powerful Lester family. This could be bloody awkward!

"Your servant, Mistress Catherine," William said, reluctantly removing his hands from around her waist and lifting her fingers to his lips.

"How do you do, sir?" she replied softly, dipping him a curtsy, then standing to look up at the tall, well-built man with hair the yellow of ripening wheat. She could feel the color still warming her cheeks, but her green eyes didn't waver from the blue intensity of his. This was the first time her waist had been encircled by a man's hands, and with an odd tingling through her, she could still feel the lean, gentle strength of them pressing into her flesh. He was handsome in a rather hawkish way. Yes, a hawk, a blond hawk, that's what he reminded her of: swift, sure, a little arrogant, even, he would be king of whatever he chose. But she sensed he would not destroy needlessly, and just as the hawk was fiercely gentle and protective of his family, so would this William be, with those he loved. Love! she chided herself in silent sarcasm. What do you know about the love of a man? She suddenly shivered and didn't know why.

William watched her openly across the table in the small, semiprivate alcove the tavern keeper had prepared for them. Every man was craning his neck to get a look at the green-eyed, black-haired beauty. She is beautiful, he thought. But it goes deeper than that. There is something special . . . a natural grace . . . an honesty, that's what it is. She has the naïveté of the convent-bred young lady, as to worldly knowledge, but she isn't shy, or coy, and thanks be to God, she doesn't simper or flutter her eyelashes! She's like a young fledgling, eager to meet and embrace life, and I'd like to be the one —the only one—to teach her! He'd known many a woman, and had become extremely adept at avoiding any serious entanglements, but never had he felt he wanted to *protect* a young lady, as he did this lovely Catherine Birchmont. Conversely, even as he wanted to protect her, he wanted her in his bed. . . .

Catherine looked around curiously, craning her neck a little to peer out into the main room, filled with men taking their breakfast of ale and bread and cheese. This was the first time she'd been in a tavern, and for the first time in her life she was breaking bread in the company of *men*, and it gave her a feeling of being a grown woman, embarking on an exciting adventure. Aware, suddenly, that the men were peering back at her, she settled around on the bench and concentrated on the sumptuous breakfast of curds and cream, eggs bubbling in butter, with thick slices of ham and the whitest bread she'd ever seen. She felt a little awkward using the new French fork Lord Birchmont had given her, used as she was to wooden spoons, or fingers, except on special occasions when there were visitors to the nunnery. For the past three years the meals at St. Clements had been very frugal, and she soon forgot her awkwardness and ate with the hearty appetite of a healthy young woman. She looked up, after a time, to find everyone staring at her, and she felt the heat rising in her face.

"I . . . I was hungrier than I thought," she said with a laugh. It had been on the tip of her tongue to comment on the unusually rich meal, but she remembered in time that although she was convent-educated, she was supposed to have been raised in a household of wealth and should be no stranger to such food. She sensed, rather than heard, her uncle's sigh of relief.

Henry, her uncle's manservant, headed the party, followed by Lord Birchmont, then Catherine, who was protected by William, and the groom, Tim, brought up the rear with the extra saddle horse tied onto his horse. But it was a different-looking Catherine now, and William kept looking over at her as if he couldn't believe the change. Whenever she caught his eye, she grinned and chuckled to herself. At her uncle's insistence she had changed into a pair of his trews, at the Blue Swan, and also donned a pair of his high soft leather boots, turned down at the top to form a cuff, and one of his white linen shirts belted around the waist twice to take up the slack and keep from losing the trews. With her hair pinned up under the flat velvet cap with a curled peacock feather, she looked like a handsome slim young boy riding astride the big brown roan, and it gave her a wild sense of freedom . . . freedom of action . . .

freedom of speech . . . freedom from the awkward, mincing airs of a young lady of quality, which she found difficult to assume.

They rode single file down Petergate to King's Square, then down The Shambles, street of the butchers, where great slabs of meat were displayed in the recessed windows and on the hooks above. The overhanging buildings on the charming medieval street and its east–west position kept the meat in the shade most of the day, but the smell of blood and the masses of hungry buzzing flies made Catherine's stomach churn with nausea. She was glad when they reached the fascinating bustle of Newgate Market. This was where she had always stolen a few irresistible moments whenever she was on an errand for the Abbess, and it had seemed, to her young, inexperienced eyes, that one must be able to buy anything in the world in the bright jumble of luxurious shops and open stands. Then they were on Ousegate and over the bridge of the quiet, meandering Ouse River, rippled with the golden sheen of the morning sun, its brown banks splattered with young pale green grass and the brilliant royal purple of loosestrife. They clattered off the bridge and onto Micklegate, passing the renowned church of St. John the Evangelist, at the foot of the hill; St. Martin-cum-Gregory, halfway up, and then, ahead of them, was the imposing Holy Trinity Church, at the top. Lost in her musing, Catherine saw but didn't immediately register the unpleasant scene in the oak-shaded square fronting Holy Trinity. When it finally penetrated, she turned with a gasp and galloped back, throwing her party into complete disarray.

"Stop it! Stop it, you little beasts!" she shouted, sliding to the ground and scattering the five half-grown boys and girls who had been throwing rocks at a young man and woman imprisoned in the stocks in front of the church. The youngsters stood at a distance, their faces sullen, glowering at her for spoiling their morning's sport. "How dare you torment someone who can't fight back?" she demanded, stamping her foot. "You're cowards! Shame on you! Shame!" She spun around and ran toward the prisoners as William jumped off his horse and reached her side.

"Catherine! Get back on your horse. I'll handle this." He tried to catch her arm, but she jerked away and ran to the young woman. Blood from a cut on her forehead was streaming down into her eyes and her imprisoned hands were clawing the air, helpless to wipe it away. Bits of loathsome offal clung to her light brown hair and once clean garments, and she was crying in a quiet, hopeless way that wrung Catherine's heart.

"Here now, here . . ." she soothed, dabbing at the cut with a handkerchief and wiping out her eyes. She could hear William angrily routing the tormentors, who took off at a run, but one youth shouted back:

"She's a bloody thief! How cum ya wanta 'elp a bloody thief?"

"I'm not! I'm not a . . . thief!" the young girl sobbed. "I did'n' 'ave no place t'go. I slep' in a barn. The . . . the farmer said I stole some . . . eggs, but I did'n'!" Her thin shoulders shook as she laid her head down on the top of the stock, then she raised her head, and her gray eyes were bewildered. "I wuz hungry, but I did'n'! He lied! He lied cuz I would'n' . . . wouldn'n' . . . lay in the 'aystook with 'im."

"You're a good girl, I'm sure," was all Catherine could think to say.

"Here's some water." William came up beside her and poured water from his jug into a tankard, and while she held it to the lips of the young girl, who drank it greedily, he wet a square of white linen hankerchief and handed it to her.

"Thank you, William," she said, wiping the grime from the girl. Free of dirt and blood, she saw a pleasing face of a girl not more than fifteen years old. The nose was a bit broad but pert, the round gray eyes met hers without flinching, and now that she was smiling at them in her gratitude, a dimple appeared briefly in her right cheek.

"Oh . . . I thank you! Bless you f' yer kindness," she murmured, her eyes again brimming with tears.

"I wish I could do more!" Catherine cried in frustration. She turned to address William, but he was standing at the adjoining stock, talking to the burly young man while he gave him a drink of water and wiped the blood from his face.

"'e wuz only tryin' t' 'elp me." The girl nodded toward the prisoner. "He wuz passin' t' farmer's place and 'e saw t' farmer tryin' . . . tryin' . . . t' force me to t' barn. And 'e telled wha' 'e saw. But"—she sighed deeply—"we don't belong 'ere, and they believed t' farmer. They said we wuz thieves together, and 'ere I ain't never set eyes on 'im afore!"

"Catherine! William! What are you about? This is not our affair! Come away, now!" Lord Birchmont jumped down to the cobblestone square, ignoring the hand of the groom, Tim, and hurried toward them, casting an uneasy glance at the passersby now gathering in small whispering groups.

"It is our affair when helpless people are being mistreated!" she answered boldly. Inwardly she quailed before the anger in his voice, but it was a long moment before her eyes dropped. "You must have seen their tormentors, Uncle. I . . . I couldn't just ride by."

"I understand, Catherine," he said more kindly. "But these two are being punished, and we have no right to interfere with the law!"

"But it wasn't the law I was interfering with," she persisted stubbornly.

"I *know* what it was!" His voice had a sharp edge. "I also heard the boy say she was a thief."

"But she isn't a thief, Uncle John! She's only a young girl. She had no place to go, so she slept in a barn. The farmer said she stole some eggs, but she says she didn't, and . . . and . . . I believe her!"

"'ey! Wat's this? Wat's this?" A gross figure of a man made his way through the onlookers, belly first, keys jingling from the large ring held in place by a leather belt around his enormous girth. Damp spots of food down his leather jerkin and the smell of ale on his breath attested he had just breakfasted at the tavern a few doors down the opposite side of the street. "Whadda yer about?" His eyes took in the open water jug and the bloodstained handkerchiefs draped on the wooden stocks. "Ah . . . coddlin' t' thieves, be ya?"

"It's not 'coddling' to stop little beasts from stoning them!" Catherine said hotly.

"Catherine!" Her uncle's roar silenced her immediately. "My niece is endowed with a soft heart, but . . . unfortunately . . . also a lack of judgment," he said, making a concerted effort to be pleasant. "And one must humor a young lady at times."

The jailer deflated instantly, his eyes taking in the richness of the man's simple dress and that of William, who was now standing at his side, regarding him with the cold eye of the aristocrat. "Well, of course, sire . . . sires," he agreed jovially, "ladies must be 'umored, and it looks t' be 'at no 'arm's done. I wuz about t' unlock this thievin' pair, and I 'opes t' two days 'as taught 'em a lessin!" He turned the key in the lock and opened the stock holding the girl's hands and feet. She slid out and tried to stand, but fell to the ground with a moan. William hurried around and gathered her up and sat her down again on the stool.

"You'd best sit a moment. Rub your hands and feet until the numbness is gone."

"Thank you kindly, sir," she murmured with a shy smile, rubbing her hands vigorously and wincing at the returning circulation.

"Where will you go, girl?" Catherine asked, avoiding her uncle's impatient frown. "Haven't you a family?"

"No. No family. But I'll manage," she said in false cheerfulness, straightening up.

"Catherine!" her uncle had reached the end of his patience.

"What's your name?" Catherine asked hurriedly.

"Tansy, ma'am. Tansy Griffin. I'm fifteen, soon sixteen."

"Uncle John"—Catherine turned to her uncle—"can't we . . . ?"

"No! We can't take her with us, Catherine! Now get on your horse. We've lost valuable time as it is." He looked at her pleading face and said grudgingly, "Well . . . I'll give her some money. Enough to keep her until she can find work. She's a strong young lady, and should have no difficulty."

"She's branded as a thief here, and may have trouble." Catherine started slowly toward her horse.

"Sir." William turned to the older man who was digging into his purse. "If you'll allow me . . ."

"Yes, William? What is it, now?"

"I've talked to this man." He indicated the burly young prisoner who was standing to the side, rubbing his hands and legs. "His name is Frank Short, and he's from Sussex. He's a farmer. Worked a small farm, but the high rent forced him out some two months ago and he's been working around the country, looking for a permanent place."

"Yes? And what's your point, William?" he queried testily.

"If you'll allow him to ride along, and the girl too, I'm sure I can find a place for both of them at Fair Meadows."

Lord Birchmont stared at him, astounded. "Have you lost your senses, William?" he demanded in a sibilant whisper. "What do you know of these two? They could be . . . be . . . cutthroats!"

"I questioned him closely. He couldn't know the answers unless he was telling the truth. And . . . we both know the landlord who forced him out. Lord Mellon."

"Oh." The name had its desired effect, and the older man's irritation drained away. "Lord Mellon. Hmmmmm! Well, I guess the young man has suffered enough," he admitted reluctantly. "But . . . they have no horses."

"He has two. The girl can ride his saddle horse. She's light-weight."

"Very well, William," he said with a sigh. "I can see I'm no match for the two of you. Tell the man to get his horses, and let's be off." He strode to his mount, shaking his head as he looked at the beaming face of his niece. He stopped abruptly and looked from the girl, Tansy, to the man, Frank, who were both watching, still wide-eyed at the sudden turn in their fortunes. "How do you know they want to come . . . want to work for your father?"

"Oh yes, sir!" Tansy answered breathlessly. "I wo' go anywhere from 'ere. I mean—" She stopped in confusion. "I mean I does want to work. An' I'm a good worker. M' mother taught me to cook 'n' sew real fine, and I'm strong"—she made a muscle of her thin arm —"see?"

Frank Short waited until she was through, watching her through patient dark eyes, and then said in a slow, hesitant voice, "I would be pleased t' work for so fine a gentleman. I wo' gi' him an honest day's work."

"Very well. Very well!" Lord Birchmont said gruffly as the groom gave him a leg up. "Now let's be off! You two can catch up with us!"

As they passed through Micklegate Bar, Catherine looked back over her shoulder for a moment. It was symbolic, somehow. As she passed through this ancient gate, she was leaving the past behind and entering a new, strange, and exciting period of her life. Would it be a life of happiness and love? She briefly closed her eyes in a silent prayer, only to see the face of William as if it were permanently burned into her eyelids. Her eyes flew open and she turned to face the road to London. There was a smile on her face, a song of happiness singing through her. She was looking at the future through her eyes of uncomplicated naïveté. She had no way of knowing that many times in the coming months she would know all the torments of an impossible love, the insidious fear of violent death and betrayal, and would long for the sanctuary and peace of St. Clements nunnery.

CHAPTER THREE

They were some two hours along the way when Tansy and Frank caught up with the party, much to Catherine's relief since she'd almost given up looking over her shoulder for sight of them. They had both taken time enough to make themselves more presentable. Tansy wore a clean but faded blue dress and had washed her hair, which was still damp, parted in the middle, and tied back with a piece of tattered ribbon, and her smiling countenance was marred only by the large bruised welt on her forehead. Frank Short looked a different person from the grimy one imprisoned in the stocks, and Catherine decided she liked the serious stocky young redhead—even his freckles looked honest—and found herself happy that the two were traveling with them to London.

Lord Birchmont had described this stretch of the Great North Road they were now traveling on as rather dull. It had taken the Romans thirty-two years to build it, in the most direct line from London up to York and on up to Newcastle-on-Tyne. It lacked the hilliness of York, but its very look of calm English permanence appealed to something inside her. The flatter fields, for miles and miles, were carefully tilled and planted with crops that created a patchwork design in varying shades of lovely soft greens, and occasionally she caught the breathtaking sight of brilliant rough-headed poppies in the corn. But she knew this splash of red beauty had its darker side, since it meant damage to the crop and less money for the farmer.

Here and there along the road she glimpsed miniature scenes, like precious vignettes to pleasure the eye: an old barn weathered to a silver gray alongside a stone cottage covered on one side with masses of pink roses; a young barefoot boy running free through a field of clover and yellow crowsfoot; a horse nuzzling her leggy colt. The cottage might be dirty and squalid inside; the boy might be running away from his chores; the colt might soon be sold away from its mother, but Catherine didn't want to think so. In the mellow golden sunshine everything took on a clean, happy orderliness, fairylike in its comely beauty.

A dark shadow suddenly fell over the land. Catherine looked up and frowned to see masses of black clouds moving swiftly across the sky, blotting out the blue. Almost immediately there was the first majestic roll of thunder, followed by a sizzling zigzag of lightning, and then the rain came down in heavy, unrelenting cold sheets, soaking them to the skin, all in a matter of minutes. The roads, dry and dusty a short time before, became slippery with greasy mud. They slogged along in silent misery for what seemed an interminable length of time.

They finally found shelter at the Truesdale Arms, an inn that was strung out along the road, seemingly in the middle of nowhere, flanked by three squeezed-together shops and two ramshackle pubs. On the opposite side of the road was a small stone church, gray and desolate in the dismal downpour. The lych-gate was open to the graveyard, where old, time-pitted headstones, half hidden in an overgrowth of weeds and willow herb, leaned to the push of the many winds. William helped Catherine down from her horse, and she had to bite her lips to keep from crying out. Every bone and muscle throbbed like individual toothaches, and she felt as if she'd been riding on a barrel and her legs had solidified in a permanent hoop. The mud hung heavy on her clothes, and she could feel the slime between her toes with every sodden step. In spite of the acute discomfort she forced herself to walk unaided. The interior of the inn was a pleasant surprise. The hard earthen floor was strewn with clean sand instead of many layers of rushes, fresh on top but covering up the filth and vermin of years underneath. The walls had been newly whitewashed, and the mighty, rough oaken beams were blackened with the curing smoke of a century or two. A cheerful fire burned in the large open-manteled fireplace in the common room, where some ten or twelve men and one woman were eating and drinking and playing darts.

A young boy, face flushed with the heat, stood before the fire-place turning a succulent leg of beef or venison on the spit. Occasionally the oozing juices missed the drip pan, popping and sizzling in the flames, and the delectable smell made her weak in the knees.

Both of the innkeeper's daughters were black-eyed and rosy-cheeked, with full figures that threatened to overflow the rounded necklines of their tight claret-colored bodices as they leaned over William, more often than necessary, while serving supper later that evening in the common room.

Catherine toyed with her food and tried not to keep glancing at William, who sat opposite her. How can one *not* look at him? she asked herself in exasperation, determinedly keeping her eyes riveted on the metal plate. She'd thought him handsome, clad as he had been this morning in the more practical dress of the traveler, with the long jerkin of soft leather, laced up the front, long tights, and high leather boots. But tonight when he walked into the common room every man had looked and envied his elegant, healthy virility. His fine white linen shirt was embroidered in scarlet silk, with a fine thread of gold repeating the pattern, and over a short scarlet velvet doublet, also embroidered in gold, he wore a pale chamois jerkin, with tights and hose of the same chamois color. But it was his finely molded mouth her eyes kept straying to, much to her chagrin.

She watched Gretchen, who paid particular attention to William, and it angered her that William didn't turn away in disgust. Every time the girl leaned over or brushed against his shoulder or his arm, he looked long and hard at the swell of her white breasts, then he would look across at Catherine, his smoldering eyes briefly tracing the outline of her square-necked green gown. It was as if he were wondering how she would compare with Gretchen, and Catherine found herself glancing down nervously to see if she was well covered. She was, but the knowledge gave her small comfort. She felt as if she were two different beings: one body but two minds, each fighting for supremacy, and totally incapable of being fused into one. One mind, steeped in the straight-laced tenets of her convent background, looked askance at those who sought the pleasures of the flesh, but her other mind led her in forbidden paths. She imagined William's hands caressing her, and his beautiful, sensuous mouth on hers. She started to tremble, and a soft gasp escaped her lips.

"Catherine? Are you all right, my dear?" Her uncle looked at her over a forkful of beef dripping with juices.

"Yes. If you'll excuse me now, Uncle John. I am a little tired."

William was immediately at her side. "I'll see you to your room, Mistress Catherine."

"Please don't bother." Her voice was cool and polite. She tried to sweep ahead of him, but his hand was like a metal trap clamped on her elbow.

"No bother."

"You're hurting my arm," she murmured under her breath as they left the room.

"Sorry," he said without releasing the pressure, marching her up the stairs, which were barely wide enough for the two to walk abreast. As they reached the narrow hallway on the second floor, he swung her smartly around to face him. "What is it, Catherine? All evening you've looked as if you'd been sucking something sour!"

"I don't know what you mean!" she replied icily, with a strange falling sensation in her stomach.

He gave her a rude shake. "Don't be a hypocrite! You're not the type to play silly, coy games!"

"No!" she snapped. "I should leave that to an *expert!*"

He looked down at her for a long moment, still holding her by the arms. His eyes narrowed. "So you think I'm playing games?" The softness of his voice was edged with a biting sarcasm.

"The game I suppose every man plays!" she flared in a true MacRaeggan temper, forgetting her vow to act like a lady, "When . . . when there's a little harlot baring her breasts like—like oysters on the half shell!"

"Like . . . like . . . oysters . . . !" he gave a strangled bark of laughter then, abruptly, his face sobered and his blue eyes gleamed with devilish glee as he tightened his grip on her arms. "You like being the center of attention, don't you, young mistress Catherine? It's new to you, I can see that. But you *revel* in it! And you don't like a man admiring another woman's . . . uh . . . attributes when he's in your company!"

"Attributes!" she scoffed, trying in vain to pull away from him. "I don't call those attributes!"

"You're jealous, little one, and it's a new experience, isn't it?"

"Jealous! I'm *disgusted!*"

His face darkened with anger and his eyes were like two pieces of hard blue flint. "Why, you little prude!" he whispered between clenched teeth. "You petty little prude! What do you expect a man to do? Turn away? A man with any blood in his veins enjoys looking! And any man who denies it is a liar or a fool! And I'm neither! I'd far rather be in the company of a soft, laughing woman who pleasures me than a sour little stick who thinks desires of the flesh are sinful!"

She cringed under the whip of his disdain. Every word flicked a quivering nerve. She wanted to cry out that what he said was true! She was jealous of the way he looked at Gretchen, and this was a feeling completely alien to her. She'd never been jealous when she'd seen a village girl in a pretty dress, or laughing with a young man. This feeling that tore at her insides like white-hot claws and left her shaken and frightened by its intensity was new to her. She hated the feeling, and anger at her own weakness made her glare back at him.

A muscle rippled along his jaw and his mouth thinned to a hard line. "You're a beautiful, bright young woman. Too beautiful and perhaps too bright. But that's not enough! You have a lot to learn, Catherine. A man wants *warmth* from a woman! He wants to hold a warm, yielding woman in his arms . . . not a cold, unresponsive statue! I wonder . . ." He gazed down at her intently. "Are you capable of warmth, Catherine?"

Her body became taut and rigid, and she felt a sudden nervous stroke of her heart. She tried to look away but couldn't. Her mind flashed a frantic warning, but she was incapable of obeying it. His eyes locked with hers, and slowly, inexorably, he crushed her close in his arms. Her head swam with an onrush of faintness as she felt the lean male strength of him, and then she was swept along on a wild and beautiful storm cloud as his warm, firm lips brushed soft kisses into the hollow of her throat, behind her ears, across her cheeks, at the pulse throbbing at her temple, then claimed her mouth in a long, passionate kiss. His lips parted and his tongue played and teased, circling the sensitive inner edge of her lips. Trembling and shaken, she tried to turn her head, tried to break free, and finally, with a low cry, she welcomed his passion. Her arms encircled his neck and her lips moved eagerly under his.

"Catherine! Catherine! You're a woman and a half! I knew it! I sensed it!" he breathed hotly against her ear as he gathered her even closer, cradling her against his broad chest, smothering her face, her hair with urgent kisses.

The frantic warnings beating against the door in her mind abruptly broke through and she shoved him away. "No! No, William! This is wrong! Wrong! Please . . ." Her voice broke and she finished in a whisper, "I . . . I . . . want to go to . . . my room."

He made a move as if to take her again in his arms, then let his hands drop and stood aside for her to pass, still fighting for breath. He turned and led the way down the narrow passageway. She hurried after him in a daze, completely disoriented, wanting to cry . . . to laugh . . . wanting to feel the muscular strength of his arms, the fiery heat of his lips on hers. He knocked briefly on the door before opening it.

"Come in! Come in!" Tansy got up from the bench before the fire and came toward them. Her wise round eyes quickly assessed the situation from Catherine's disheveled appearance and the grimness of William's expression.

"I were jus' goin' down to fetch a posset fer us, Miss Catherine. Be back in a flip." She eased past them, her back to Catherine, and gave William an impish grin before hurrying to the back stairs.

He stood for a moment regarding her, his expression unreadable, and she became still, utterly still to her innermost core. "Good night, Catherine," he said with a slight inclination of his head.

"Good night, William," she murmured, still staring at him. Her creamy white skin was flushed with color, her black hair, pulled from confining ribbon ties, hung past her shoulders in a glorious silken mass, her soft red mouth was slightly parted, showing the edge of even white teeth, her high, thrusting breasts moved up and down in agitated rapidity. Never had he seen her more beautiful and desirable. But it was the expression in her eyes, her great green eyes, that hit him like a blow in the stomach. In their wide-eyed innocence they regarded him with a mixture of fear and wonder. He was sure now that this really was her first experience with a man's passion, perhaps even her first kiss and she was frightened and startled at her response.

He cursed himself for being too eager, for forgetting the proprieties. What was he thinking of to take such liberties with a young innocent girl, of an impeccable background . . . the niece of his father's close friend . . . as he would a common trollop! But the very look of her sent the blood coursing madly through his veins and broke down all the silly walls of convention. He caught her hand and raised it to his lips. "Rest well. I'll see you in the morning, Catherine." He smiled pleasantly and went out, closing the door behind him.

"Thank you. Rest well," she said numbly to the closed door. She took a few steps, as if to follow him, then, with a low cry, sagged against the rough wood. She was still trembling as if she had a bad chill, but it wasn't a chill she felt, it was more like a fever. She could still feel the heat of his mouth, the pressure of his arms, the lean strength of his body. "Catherine! Catherine! What's *happening* to you? Have you no shame?" she groaned, pounding the door with her fists. "The first young man of your acquaintance! A man you've known for one short day! One day! Oh!"

Catherine was propped up in the bed when Tansy returned with two steaming possets made from hot milk, laced with beaten eggs, cinnamon, ale, and sugar. Also on the tray were some slices of cheese and brown bread and a fruity-looking chunk of cake.

"Oh, wonderful, Tansy! Thank you!" she cried, clapping her hands in delight. "I'm starved! I just wasn't . . . hungry . . . at sup-

per. Bring the stool over and put the tray on the bed, Tansy." She
pushed the cover aside and sat up, tailor-fashion, patting the edge of
the bed.

The girl happily complied, and soon, with mouths stuffed, they
were freely exchanging confidences as new acquaintances, drawn to
each other, invariably do. Tansy had been born in London, her father had died in debtors' prison, and her mother had died of the
sweating sickness a year ago. She'd gone to an aunt in Selby, who'd
treated her so badly she ran away. Since then she'd worked and
slept where she could, lashed by the hands and tongues of dried-out,
penurious housewives, scorned by their daughters, and plagued by
the eager, groping hands of the young men of the families.

"But none of 'em tumbled me! I kep' what I 'as!" She sighed and
shrugged her thin shoulders. "Sometimes I used ter wonder w'at I
were savin' it fer! But . . . now . . ." she smiled, keeping her eyes
lowered, while two pink spots colored her cheeks.

"I think Frank is very nice!" Catherine said with a knowing grin.

Tansy's head jerked up and her eyes were wide with consternation. "How . . . did yer know I . . . I were thinkin' o' Frank?"

"Because I've seen you looking at him when he wasn't looking.
And I've seen him do the same to you."

"An' . . . an' what did 'e look like . . . when he were lookin'?"
she asked with a nervous little catch to her voice.

"He liked what he saw . . . very much!"

"Aw!" She dismissed it casually, but her eyes were shining and
she finished her posset in thoughtful, contented silence. Catherine
looked up to find she was being gravely assessed by two round gray
eyes.

"Yer sweet on Mister William!" A statement rather than a question, and before Catherine could gather her startled wits, she said,
"Yer got kissed. Did yer like it?"

"I . . . I . . ." Denial was on the tip of her tongue, but as she
looked into the eyes of her new friend she saw only open, honest curiosity. "Yes," she replied softly. "Yes, I . . . I liked it. It was the
first time."

"Aw! Sommone as pretty as you!"

"I was raised in a convent," she reminded her quietly.

"Aw, sure!" She slapped her forehead with an open palm. "I for-got! Well"—a frown creased her sunburned brow—"them two daughters sure ain't been raised in a convent! They jus' acts like they wants ter giv't away!" She glanced worriedly toward the win-dow. "I just hopes they don'—" She broke off as she glanced at Catherine's frozen face, recalling the sight, earlier that evening, of Gretchen leaning over the handsome Mister William with bold fa-miliarity. She groped clumsily around for something to say to erase that look from her beautiful friend's face, and she started to regale her with stories of thieves and pickpockets she'd seen, stories of brash highway robbers—about the criminal complicity of some un-scrupulous innkeepers who, for a cut of the loot, tipped off the rob-bers to wealthy guests who were traveling the road alone.

"They wuz one innkeeper who wuz 't worst of all!" she said in a conspiratorial whisper. "'e 'ad a single bed in a upstair' room. Under it were a big trapdoor. When the gentleman were asleep, t' trapdoor were open' an' t' bed felled down into a big tub o' boilin' water. The gent were kilt, 'is 'orse an' valubles takened away in t' night, and no one never knew wha' 'appened to t' gent!"

"Oh, Tansy! You're making it up!" Catherine laughed with a deli-cious shiver of excitement, hugging her knees to her chest.

"That's t' way it were telled t' me!" she insisted as the two young girls grinned at each other. Tansy was content. Laughter had erased that troubled look from her lovely friend's eyes.

In spite of the changeable weather they made surprisingly good time in the days that followed. Twice they lost their way in the teeming rain and took a wrong turn because one road's morass looked no different from another. They were plagued with gnats from the undrained marshes and they had to keep a sharp eye out for the many potholes, where a horse could break its leg. When the muddy roads dried out, the dust rose, covering them with a fine, choking powder that lined their noses and mouths and reddened their eyes. But in spite of it all Catherine was enjoying the adven-ture and William's good humor and sprightly conversation. Ever since the night at the Truesdale Arms his conduct had been meticulously proper, as he pointed out places of interest and concerned himself, in a friendly way, for her comfort. Even Lord Birchmont had relaxed his vigil. Conversely, Catherine found herself a little piqued that William no longer regarded her with burning desire, and then she had to laugh at herself for her contrariness.

They were a few miles from the small village of Welwyn and it was fast growing dark when Frank, spearheading the group, halooed them to stop. They could see the darker outline of a cart stuck in the mud and the one horse struggling valiantly to move the impossible burden. William was already off his horse when Lord Birchmont reluctantly instructed his men to the farmer's aid. As the men bent to their muddy task, seven horsemen rode swiftly down on them from a large copse of trees, handkerchiefs hiding the lower part of their faces.

"Don't draw or you're dead," the leader shouted as they surrounded the travelers. "Get down off your horses and empty your pockets and be quick about it!" His wave encompassed Lord Birchmont and the two girls. "And you!" he addressed William, "stay right where you are! Move your hands one inch and I'll cut them off."

Catherine felt as if she were caught helpless and speechless in a frightening nightmare. The scene had a weird, unreal quality about it: night hadn't completely settled in, and black clumps of trees along the road were silhouetted against the rain-drenched murkiness; the four men of their party were dark statues near the farmer's cart, and sooty, shadowy figures of the highwaymen moved swiftly and silently in a well-organized plan. Three helped the "farmer" unload the huge rocks from the cart, which had been covered by produce, and threw them to the side of the road. The horse pulled the empty cart out of the ruts and the animal was unhitched and saddled, while the cart was abandoned alongside the rocks. "Let's make sure you both don't have something hidden under your hats!" With a quick flick of his sword the leader sent Lord Birchmont's hat flying, then Catherine's. Her hair, held on top of her head by two makeshift pins, fell in a shimmering mass around her shoulders.

"Great hopping Harry! It's a woman! And what a woman!" he

chortled exultantly, peering at her through the gloom. With his free hand he pulled his kerchief down around his neck and jerked her to him by the hair, crushing her against his chest, his fingers still entwined in the silken strands. "It's been a long time since I kissed a real lady!" Then his hot, wet lips were bruising her mouth with punishing savagery. She fought like a wildcat, scratching and kicking, and when his lips came down again on hers she sank her teeth into his lower lip, and with a scream of rage he released her, flinging her to the ground. Then Tansy jumped on his back, pounding him with her fists and yelling like a banshee.

William took advantage of the diversion to scoop up his sword and, roaring with fury, he cleared the distance in a few strong leaps. "Take your filthy hands off her!" he bellowed as he swung his sword up for the plunge. His upraised arm remained motionless for a split second while an expression of stunned surprise registered on his face, then he fell face down in the muck, a knife protruding from his back, thrown by the nearest outlaw.

CHAPTER FOUR

They were nearing London, and from the hill, in the gray of the morning's first light, the distant city was a huddled hodgepodge of dark gray buildings interwoven by the serpentine gleam of the mighty Thames River. Outside Barnet, they had left behind the sleeping villages and the fragrant fields of lavender and thyme and joined the growing lines of farmers and the king's men who would be patrolling the highway until the sun came up.

The Highgate Road was choked with lumbering wagons and carts piled high with produce—or filled with the cackle-and-honk of poultry for the city's markets—and bawling droves of cattle and sheep for the slaughter pens of Smithfield. It hadn't rained for two days and the dust was suffocating, but Catherine was little aware of anything but William's inert form in the cart beside her. No matter what care was taken to cushion the shock of riding in a cart, Catherine could see William wince every time the crude wheels hit a bone-shaking stretch of rocks. He'd been flushed and feverish and muttering incoherently for the past eight or ten hours, and although she kept sponging his hot head and hands with the dusty brown water and forcing spoonfuls of the medicine mixed for them by the apothecary, it all seemed to little avail.

When the cart rattled through the old Roman wall at Alder's Gate, they left the horror of Smithfield behind and entered the familiar bustle of a big city. This is London! This is to be my home! she cried silently, with a surge of excitement mixed with a sense of tremendous relief that at last William would receive the care of highly skilled physicians and she would be able to soak for hours and hours in a tub of hot water and rid herself, finally, of the layers of dirt that seemed to have permeated her very bones.

London was made up of two separate cities: this City of London, which was a square mile of teeming thousands and fantastic riches, enclosed within the old Roman wall; and west, down the Thames, was the second city: Westminster, considered to be a part of London. Connecting the two was a row of great riverside mansions, with beautiful gardens that ran from the Strand—a road paralleling the Thames—right down to the riverbank.

The London roads were narrow, dirty, bumpy, and noisy with people, horses, and the rumble and clatter of carts, and Cheapside Road was a jumble of pubs, shops, and market stalls, reminding her of a larger Newgate Market. But the sights and sounds were music to her eyes and ears after Smithfield.

Then they reached the Thames, rippling and gleaming in the morning sunshine, stretched out to either side of them like curved flowing arms beckoning the adventurer to unknown and fascinating places. Hundreds of wherries and other small boats for hire plied the river along with the slower private and commercial barges. Many were wind-powered, and the bright sails fluttered and billowed in the brisk morning breeze. To the east she could see the outline of London Bridge, the only one to span the Thames, with its piers supporting the nineteen stone arches and one wooden drawbridge. Near the bridge were several large seagoing ships riding at anchor, and on the rise of a hill she caught a glimpse of the forbidding Tower of London, which sent a sudden shiver down her back. On both sides of the Thames buildings were lined up so closely they seemed to be elbowing one another out of the way, fighting for breathing space. Here and there the spires of a church or castle turrets jutted high and haughty above their plebian neighbors.

They boarded Lord Birchmont's barge and moved up the Thames, past Whitehall Palace and Westminster, with homes of great and important men sandwiched in between; and then they were at the Chelsea landing of Birchmont Hall.

Lady Mary Birchmont smiled at Catherine, but the warmth didn't reach her brown watchful eyes. She appeared about to embrace her, but her eyes flicked nervously over the girl's soiled, wrinkled clothing and she leaned over and gave her a birdlike peck on the cheek. "We hope you'll be happy with us, here."

Catherine curtsied, feeling a little foolish in trews and boots. "Thank you . . . ma'am. I'm sure I will." She took Tansy by the arm. "This is Tansy Griffin, my . . . maid." She felt somewhat dishonest introducing her thus, but her uncle had requested she do so, to save questions.

"How do, mum?" Tansy curtsied nicely.

"How do you do, Tansy?" Her eyes moved over the girl and immediately discarded her.

The manicured expanse of lawn felt like spongy velvet under her tired feet, glossy ivy grew up the huge elms that dappled the lawn with late afternoon shade, the white froth of hawthorn still decorated the hedges down the distant sides of the grass, marking the boundaries of Birchmont Hall. Lofty cedars were clumped at either side of the house, their dark majesty throwing into relief the bright masses of streaked gillyflowers, tiger lilies, lavender, and the pink and creamy beauty of the damask and moss roses that wafted delicate fragrance into the air.

It's a different world! Catherine thought as she stood still for a moment, looking at the beautiful three-story house set like a deep rose jewel on the rise of the green slope. A clean, perfumed, worry-free world where no one need go hungry or be concerned with the cesspool around them! And I'm to be a part of this world, and at the thought, she was assailed with a sudden, unexplainable sense of fear.

At her side, Tansy gave a deep sigh of wonder, and Catherine turned to her with a smile. "It's a beautiful house, isn't it?"

"Gor! I ain' never seen nothin' like it!"

"Father! Father! You're home!" Sheila came flying out the door and flung herself at him. "What did you bring me?" She was immediately engrossed in examining the jeweled pin her besotted father had managed to hide from the highwaymen, and was completely unaware and uncaring of anyone else. With a sinking heart Catherine studied her lovely pale yellow sheer gown and matching shoes. The yellow headdress almost looked like a halo on top of the dark gold hair that fell down her back in shining order. She looked so fresh and cool and feminine it made Catherine even more painfully conscious of her own smelly, dirty appearance.

Sheila glanced away from her pin briefly as her father made the introductions, then her eyes instantly swiveled back. She gaped at her in disbelief, and a shadow of distaste was wiped away by her burst of derisive laughter.

Catherine lifted her head arrogantly. "Do you find my appearance amusing?"

"I . . . was expecting a . . . a girl, and you look like . . . like . . ." she gasped.

"An unkempt, unwashed man?" Catherine finished for her icily.

There was a glacial silence while Sheila glared at her with sullen hostility, then she gave her a mock-rueful smile. "I'm truly sorry, cousin Catherine. That was a very poor welcome, indeed. Now"— she touched her on the shoulders and brushed her lips quickly against her cheek—"welcome to our home. It's your home, too, now."

"We've had a long and difficult trip, daughter," her father said quietly. "Catherine dressed like that at my request—for our safety on the road. As it was, we were robbed and William was badly hurt."

"William! William was hurt? Where is he?" Her face flushed with color and her brown eyes were alight with eagerness, giving beauty and vitality to her delicate features. Scarcely waiting for an answer, she picked up her skirts and ran across the driveway and disappeared through the open door.

Her mother looked after her with indulgent eyes, then turned to her husband with a smile. "Well . . . you know, John, how they feel about each other!" She glanced over at Catherine as if to make sure she understood the situation. "I wouldn't be surprised . . ." She left the thought dangling.

Catherine felt a jolt of resentment. So that's how it was! But of course! What could be more natural—uniting two wealthy, titled families! Now she understood her uncle's nervous concern whenever William paid her too much attention! Her resentment deepened. William wouldn't have dared take the liberties with Sheila that he had with her, the poor relation! And how little it actually meant to him! Vowing to avoid his company as much as possible, she blindly followed after Tansy as Lady Birchmont led them across a cobbled drive and into a little anteroom of the house. It was built in bold innovation in the form of a three-story cube with recessed L-shaped wings extending out on either side of the house and meeting at a back gate on the Strand side. The wings were only one-story high and the width of one room all around, forming an open courtyard on both sides of the three-story cubed structure.

Double doors opened into the Great Hall from the anteroom, and Catherine stood still, looking around at the display of wealth, thrilled in spite of the waves of weariness washing over her. The lofty ceiling was decorated with a flower design pressed into cream-colored plaster touched with gold, obviously the creation of an Italian artisan. The walls and doors were of polished oak and hung floor to ceiling with rich Cloth of Arras tapestries, colorfully depicting hunting and battle scenes. The floor was a patterned slate, as was the huge fireplace, before which stood two large carved Bishop's throne chairs, a sure sign of wealth. A gigantic table centered the wide hall, with a dozen small, stiff chairs along the sides. Without doubt the carved chairs would grace the head and foot at mealtimes, for Lord Birchmont and his lady. There were blue velvet pads on the recessed seats of the two bay windows, which were set within a frame and divided horizontally by transoms and vertically by stone mullions. Stained glass in the colors of gold, blue, and rose filled in the arch of the windows, and the afternoon sun decorated the floor with the colored patterns.

As Catherine gazed up at the beautiful staircase of polished wood that disappeared into the second floor, she had a mental picture of Tansy and her standing in the midst of all this luxury, looking like two awestruck, disreputable waifs who should have been shown the servants' entrance, and she had to stifle a crazy desire to laugh. She got silly this way when she was overly tired and emotionally drained, and the silliness always verged on tears.

Sheila had been turned away earlier at William's door, but now, at her knock, she was bade to enter. The curtains were drawn against the sun, and in the rue-fragrant dimness she could see an elderly servant woman sitting primly on a stool and the physician, Sir Howard Walker, bending over the patient in the large canopied bed. She curtsied slightly to the physician and looked down on the man she planned to marry if at all possible. Sir Howard had carefully placed the raw flesh of a freshly killed and gutted pigeon over the wound and he was securing it in place with a bandage circling his chest, then he turned him on his side. Sheila shuddered inwardly at the sight of two blood-swollen leeches on William's forehead and two near the wound, drawing out the fevered blood, but she managed not to let her revulsion show.

"Dear William!" she said softly, putting one hand delicately on her chest as if she were almost overcome with feeling. "I'm so relieved to see you looking so well. I had such frightening visions of you at death's door! I would have been"—she paused, lowering her eyes—"*devastated* if anything happened to you."

"Thank you, Sheila," he said with a weak grin. "I'm glad to be alive!" He frowned and tried to raise up on one elbow but was pushed back down by Sir Howard. "Catherine? Where's Catherine, Sheila? Is she all right?"

"Catherine?" Her head snapped up, and like a wild animal, she was instantly alert to the danger of a trespasser on her chosen domain. "Oh, cousin Catherine. Yes, she's fine, William. She was rather a surprise—looking for all the world like a man—but she's fine!" She couldn't quite manage to wash all the acid out of her reply.

He smiled, and even in the dimness she could see the tender expression. "That's good. I'm glad. She had a rough time."

She made light small talk, catching him up on the doings of the court and mutual friends, then, begging to be excused for fear of tiring him and promising to be happily at his beck and call whenever he wished, she left the room, smiling sweetly back at him over her shoulder.

She wanted to slam the door, she wanted to scream and kick things, but most of all she wanted to rake her fingernails down the pretty face of her new cousin. Even with those ugly man's clothes on, nothing could hide her beautiful features. He's never looked at me like that! Never! William is mine! Mine! And she's not going to get him! she vowed in hysterical vehemence as she flung herself face down on her bed and beat at it with frantic fists.

Sheila wasn't prepared for the full scope of her beauty, nor was Lady Birchmont, and even Lord Birchmont—having seen her for many days in men's clothing, with a hat covering her glorious hair —had almost forgotten how breathtaking she was as a woman. Holding the skirt of her dress up slightly, Catherine seemed to float down the staircase, looking every inch the lady to the manor born. Lady Birchmont gave her daughter an oblique glance. Sheila's lips were set in a smile, but her dark eyes glittered dangerously. She knew that look: a forced cordiality masking an inner fury, and the older woman felt a wave of bitter animosity toward this new member of their home, and vexation at her husband's poor timing. Why couldn't he have left her at St. Clements at least until Sheila and William were safely married? It was going to be difficult at best since William didn't seem to feel any inclination toward marriage . . . as yet.

The animosity of Lady Birchmont and Sheila was so thinly veiled by smiles and casual conversation that it was almost a palpable thing, and Catherine was so uncomfortable, she scarcely knew what she was eating. The lanky white-headed physician, Sir Howard Walker, seated on her left in the immense Great Hall, paid her lavish compliments and promised to have his two lawyer sons call on her at her earliest convenience, which only served to heighten the current of resentment. Pleading weariness, Catherine escaped as soon as it was possible.

She closed the door to her bedroom and sagged against it, overwhelmed with the feeling she'd like to run from this great house and its Birchmont women, with their half-submerged animosities. She'd been so grateful, so thrilled to have a home at last, but she now realized that her uncle's hospitality and concern for her well-being weren't shared by his wife and daughter. Was it because of William? She was suddenly stricken with a feeling of mortification. William had sustained his terrible knife wound on her behalf.

I'll see him in the morning, she thought, and thank him properly . . . and I'll do everything possible to speed his recovery. How petty I'm being . . . wanting to stay out of his way because of Sheila!

Tansy had been watching her from the bench in front of the small fire, which cast its mellow glow over the large poster bed, hung with dark red silk, the linen-fold clothespress, and over the walls covered with canvas painted to look like tapestry. She had turned down the bedcovers, made up her own truckle bed, and laid out Catherine's threadbare nightgown.

Catherine peered down to see what was lying on her gown. With a small cry she picked up two pieces of dried white bell heather.

"T'ey wuz rolle' up in yer ol' nunnery dress," Tansy murmured.

"Oh, Tansy! I forgot to put a piece under Sister Emily's pillow! My uncle came and I just forgot everything else! She . . . she was like a . . . a mother to me, Tansy, and I miss her so!" The sobs came, wracking her tired body. "I thought all this"—she threw out a hand to encompass the richness—"would be enough, but it isn't, Tansy! It doesn't make up for feeling loved! And I'm not *really* a Birchmont! Not much, anyway. I'm *really* a MacRaeggan!" And while Tansy awkwardly patted her shoulder, she told her the story, as related by her uncle, swearing her to secrecy.

Sheila looked in on William, but he was sleeping soundly, watched by her old dragon of a nurse, Della, so she went on to her room. In a sudden urge to question her father more about Catherine and feel out the possibility of finding her a position elsewhere—she was well educated, so why not a governess?—she raised her hand to knock on their adjoining door, but her hand froze. The door was ajar, and her parents' voices were raised in an argument about Catherine. She put her ear to the crack.

". . . and I fail to see why you couldn't have . . . well . . . *arranged* it financially with the Abbess to keep her at St. Clements. At least until Sheila was settled!" Lady Birchmont walked around restlessly, picking up and putting down.

Lord Birchmont watched his wife's prowling and thought what a fine figure of a woman she still was in the soft flowing night-robe of rose damask and her fair hair loose down her back. She hadn't got fat, as so many women of her age did. Damned if he wouldn't pleasure himself tonight, he thought with a surge of excitement. That is, if she ever stopped talking. Reluctantly he opened his ears again.

". . . might save the situation if we married Catherine off to one of Sir Howard's sons. But you must act quickly, John. You could give her an *acceptable* dowry. I'm sure Sir Howard would be most agreeable. You saw how he was taken with her . . ."

"Madame!" he thundered, his face purpling.

Mary Birchmont instantly regretted her haste. She should have waited until later, when he was mellow and content. She'd gone too far. She had challenged his pride as a Birchmont. He was such a pain when it came to his darn family tree! His next words would be: "She's a Birchmont!"

"She's a *Birchmont!* She's not to be bundled off higgledy-piggledy to just *anyone!*"

"I was only concerned about our daughter's happiness. She's very much in love with William, as you well know. I don't want to see Sheila *hurt!*"

He rose to the bait at the mention of his beloved daughter. "Mary," he said placatingly, going to her and putting an arm around her slim waist, "I can *assure* you that William will *never* marry my niece, Catherine."

She slowly turned around, incredibility written all over her face. "How can you say that? How can you be so sure, John?"

He felt his defenses rapidly crumbling. He'd meant only himself to know Catherine's secret, but his wife would never give up as long as she considered Catherine a threat. She'd find little ways to make life a little less pleasant for her, and he truly wanted his niece to have a happy, rich life after the regimented, penurious one she'd known at St. Clements. Mary would find a way to punish him, too. She could be warm and loving when she chose. But if she didn't choose, she could be as unyielding as a ramrod, and at his age he had no desire to force himself on an unwilling, uncooperative wife. He sighed deeply.

"Her name is Catherine MacRaeggan and she's the daughter of Lady Anne MacRaeggan . . . the great-granddaughter of Lady Catherine MacRaeggan, my father's sister, and . . ."

Sheila now had to strain to hear, as her father unconsciously lowered his voice as he related the story to his wife, who was making small noises of astonishment. Sheila listened intently, with every nerve in her body, and as the minutes passed, her eyes. grew wider and wider. She cautiously pulled the door shut and ran to her bed, throwing herself face down and smothering her shouts of gleeful laughter in the pillows. She lay awake for some time, smiling into the darkness. This changed things! How it changed them! she told herself with rising exultance. I'll be the good friend and confidante to Catherine, as I'd planned. But I'll not fight William's affection for her, if that's what it will be. After all, what good would it really do if he's determined to have her? I won't have to force her to leave Birchmont because . . . she laughed aloud . . . she can never marry William, and she'll leave of her own accord! Then—she smiled triumphantly—he'll turn to me: the sweet, true-blue friend, and I'll console him. I'll *console* him right into marriage! Later, when a shaft of moonlight poured through the window on her sleeping face, she was still smiling.

CHAPTER FIVE

The next two weeks were gay and exciting for Catherine. Since the morning after her arrival Lady Birchmont and Sheila had been so sweet she could scarcely believe it. At first she thought their effusive, cordial manner smacked of pretense, but gradually she became convinced that her impression of their animosity that first night stemmed from her own fatigue and insecurity. The clothier had come from London with bolts and bolts of materials to choose from, and after she'd made her choices, two seamstresses and their helpers had stayed at the manor house for nine days, cutting, fitting, and sewing. Now she had a mind-boggling number of beautiful things: two morning dresses, three for afternoons and formal calls, two for evening dress-up, two of the most elegant ball gowns she'd ever seen, a riding costume of fine plum wool edged with plum velvet, plus a night-robe, two nightdresses, and a few undergarments. Her uncle's generosity seemed to have no bounds!

Lord and Lady Birchmont were often away—he with affairs of the king and she with the ladies of the court. She was not a lady-in-waiting to the queen, but she was often included in their leisure pastimes. And when she was "at home," Birchmont Hall was besieged with callers, many of them young gentlemen friends of Sheila, who came to see for themselves the rumored beauty of her cousin, Catherine, and remained to be drawn into her circle of admirers. They walked in the gardens, read poetry aloud, rode over the meadows and along the lanes of the rich green countryside around London, and although they often discussed the king, his new queen, and the dissolution of the monasteries, the young ladies and young gentlemen callers spoke no treasonous words and Catherine wisely kept her counsel. In the courtyard of Birchmont Hall the young gentlemen, including Gerald and Boyd Walker, the physician's two sons, were always delighted to give her lessons in bowling and archery, and they tried, in vain, to be casual about it when they slipped an arm around her waist or over her shoulder, positioning her hands on the longbow. At these times she was always conscious of William watching from his window, and later on from a chair in the garden, and although he gave no outward indication, she hoped he was piqued just a little.

One fine May morning, Lady Birchmont, Catherine, Sheila, and her maid, Hetty, left Birchmont Hall by wherry boat right after breakfast and Tim and Frank met them with the horses at the Temple Bar landing and accompanied them for their protection while they shopped. Catherine found the narrow, tangled cobweb of London's streets fascinating in spite of the mixture of evil smells and the earsplitting cacophony of noise. In the congestion progress was slow, and they rode single file, keeping their horses to the sides of the roads and alleys, near the buildings, careful to avoid the drainage gutter down the center, where whatever garbage—vegetable and human—not claimed by the quarrelsome, shrieking kites, was washed away to some unknown dark and unhealthy place. Shooting off any main thoroughfare was a maze of lanes and alleys with tall, wooden-framed houses rising on either side, story above story—leaning so far toward one another she felt as if she were passing under archways—and glimpses of the Thames down every southward-running street.

As they approached London Bridge, Catherine felt an odd sort of surprise. It didn't look like a bridge, it looked like just another narrow street, built across the Thames, lined on either side with houses and shops in various stages of disrepair.

"This will be perfect for your ball gown, Catherine, and this to wear for the Coronation," Lady Birchmont said, placing first one, then the other ornate gabled headdress on her niece, while Sheila, who'd already chosen hers, selected some fancy garters. "You young ladies are so fortunate to be able to show your lovely tresses," she sighed. "We, who need the softening look, must keep them covered, unfortunately!"

As they left the shop, they were besieged by more than a dozen of ragged, dirty youngsters who pushed and jostled them, outshouting one another, begging for coins. Tim and Frank cleared the way to their waiting horses, yelling threats and swiping at them with their whips, while Sheila and her mother walked on without hesitation, heads high and mentally holding their noses. But Catherine felt so guiltily rich, she stopped for a moment and quickly dug down into her reticule and pressed a few coins from the money her uncle had given her into the nearest grimy hands and hurried to catch up. Immediately she was attacked by the others, screaming and spitting their fury as they shoved her against the buildings, beating at her with their fists, tearing at her clothing and calling her unspeakable names. People watched from doorways, leaned from windows, and shouted obscenities at the little river rats, but no one physically interfered. Catherine at first kept her arms in front of her face, trying to fend them off, but finally she was swinging at them wildly, feeling as if she'd been thrown into a warren of vicious rats with blackened teeth and fetid breath.

Tim and Frank, with the help of the shopkeeper, succeeded in routing them, knocking them about like tenpins, but they seemed frighteningly indestructible as they popped back up on their feet and scurried away to some dark hole under the bridge. Catherine staggered to her feet and was helped back into the shop while Frank hurried away to locate an apothecary. She tried to bring some order to her disheveled appearance, but her hands were shaking so, she finally gave up and just listened to her aunt's scolding.

". . . like animals! Worse than animals! They should be swept away like dirt, along with the filth they live in! *Now* do you understand what I've been *warning* you about . . . in London? There's danger all around, and you must never stop! Never permit one to get near you!"

Catherine said nothing, just nodded her head once in a while so her aunt would know she was listening. She somehow felt no anger because she understood, in a way. That coin might have made the difference between a full or an empty stomach. It would have been better not to have given any if she couldn't give to them all. But, she thought with a spasm of shivering, I felt terror, stark terror, because they'd been all over me like a swarm of frenzied, starved gutter rats, and I was so stunned at the unexpected attack I didn't know how to fight back. But next time I'll know! But I hope there won't be a next time. To fight children—even vicious ones warped by dirt and poverty—somehow goes against my grain.

The apothecary sponged off the scratches on her hands and the long one down the side of her neck, applying salve against infection and muttering all the while about how bad conditions were getting in London and how he would be glad someday if he could find a little cottage for his family out in the country. And Catherine thought of the green peace of St. Clements and felt a sudden welling of tears stinging her eyes.

They finished their shopping, stopping at the goldsmith's while her aunt paid for a huge mirror, in an ornate gold frame, which had just arrived from Venice, Italy, and would be brought to Birchmont Hall by wherry boat. There was a large mirror in the shop, and Catherine stood before it entranced, scarcely believing the reflection that looked back at her. She'd never seen herself in a mirror; the nearest thing had been a reflection in a summer-still pool of water, or in a sheet of shiny metal.

"You're a beautiful young lady!" she heard the elderly goldsmith say as he nodded his appreciation, but she didn't move. It was the first time she'd really been *sure* she was beautiful, and it did wonderful things for her self-confidence.

Their last stop was at the cobbler's to pick up shoes that had been ordered to be made for the three of them, and then they slowly retraced their way to Cheapside. Noisy crowds glutted the square, but from the appearance of the aimless groups and the knots of talking, laughing people, a sporting event was over and they were looking for more amusement. As they picked their way through, Catherine was assaulted by a cloying, offensive odor. Tim desperately tried to turn his mount and those behind him into a side alley, but it was too late. A path seemed to peel open before them to reveal the center of the square. Between the Cheapside Cross and the fountain were two charred bodies.

Catherine tried to bring her hand up to flip the reins, to urge her horse into motion, then tried to will her head to turn from the grisly sight, but she seemed curiously atrophied and just sat there, unable to move, unable to close her eyes. Faces . . . eyes wide . . . leering faces, laughing faces . . . mocking faces . . . startled faces . . . looked up at her, but she didn't realize it was her earsplitting screams they were listening to.

Frank grabbed the reins of her mount and pulled her through the square, breaking the bonds of her paralysis and shutting off her screaming. As they passed the smoking horror, she caught a glimpse of a crude scorched sign, nailed to a nearby box, that read: "2 skots bern hear today." Skots? she wondered numbly. Oh . . . Scots . . . two Scots burn here today. . . . They'd been two Scotsmen. What deed had they done that called for such a horrible penalty? I'm a Scot! she thought as a wave of sickening anger rolled over her. I'm a MacRaeggan! And if this is what the English do . . . what they find so amusing . . . I'm proud to be a Scot! As her fury increased, she turned in the saddle and shouted at the faces looking up at her, "Did you enjoy watching them burn? Did you make it a special gay holiday? You're inhuman! You're nothing but cold-blooded beasts!" Then she fell forward in the saddle, her body wracked with great, shuddering sobs.

The house was quiet, and Tansy seemed to be sleeping soundly when Catherine, unable to rest, crept out of bed, slipped on her night-robe, and let herself out into the hall.

William slowly put down his book, Chaucer's *Parlement of Foules,* and stared at Catherine in wary surprise. Thoughts of her had been disturbing his concentration and seeing her like this was like seeing a beautiful and most welcome apparition materialize.

"Yes, Catherine?" He stood up, his voice guarded.

She came over to stand by the Erasmus chair, where he'd been seated. Her expression was troubled. "I . . . I couldn't sleep, William. May I talk to you?"

"Of course." He indicated the chair, feeling a sharp disappointment that she hadn't somehow—in some inexplicable way—been impelled to come to him imbued by the same desire he felt for her, but, conversely, he knew a feeling of relief. She wouldn't be the tantalizingly innocent and desirable young woman she was if she didn't regard her virginity as the gift to be given to the man she married.

"I'm all ears," he said, drawing the stool over near her chair, as if it were the most normal thing in the world for a young single woman to come to a gentleman's bedroom after midnight.

"I made a very unladylike spectacle of myself today," she said, "and I was taken severely to task by both my uncle and aunt—to say nothing of Sheila. But it isn't that. I suppose I've always been enough of a rebel to know that my actions will bring me criticism at times. But as long as I don't bring harm or disgrace to those I care about, I don't mind being chastised." She sat quietly as she talked, her voice almost toneless, as if she were a child reciting her sins, and he was consumed with a desire to hold and comfort her.

"What does trouble me, William"—her green eyes searched his face, and he kept his expression controlled—"I'm so full of hate inside that I can't sleep."

"Hate? For what? Whom?"

"For the *English!*" She related the events of her day in London. Told in a flat, expressionless voice, her words had a quality of naked disbelief in what she was relating. She rubbed her forehead in bewilderment.

"What's the world coming to, William? How could people watch such a heinous barbaric spectacle? How *could* they?" A flood of anger broke through her frozen façade, her voice rose, color stained her face . . . a face now strangely paradoxical, a mixture of the harsh lines of bitter fury and a hurt, childlike vulnerability.

"I looked at those coarse, avaricious faces and I *hated* the English! And I hated the *part of me* that's English!" She stopped abruptly. She couldn't retract what she'd revealed, but she couldn't recant or she'd give it too much importance.

He caught the slip but saw her immediate distress, so he didn't pursue it. He leaned over and took her hands in his. "You're *generalizing.* You 'hated the English,' you say, but that was only an infinitesmal segment of 'the English' at the burning. There are men in every country who get a thrill, a sense of satisfaction, out of watching another's suffering."

"But, why?"

He shrugged helplessly. "I don't know. Maybe it satisfies their own frustrations, makes their own miserable lot seem more bearable by comparison! But," he continued firmly, "you're forgetting the *majority* of Englishmen: the solid, kind, hardworking English, who are sickened at such brutality, who would avert their faces should they have to pass by, who would keep their children indoors, and who would change, if possible, those laws that make a mockery of life, of decency and dignity of man." They regarded one another soberly, without moving.

"You were shocked and angry," he said with a quiet smile. "Understandably so. *I* wouldn't have minded your shouting. But the Birchmonts are not used to such . . . uh . . . impulsive acts."

"Yes, I know. My aunt said she fainted at the sight, as a gentlewoman should, and Sheila professed to be faint for some time." She sat there mutely for a long moment, staring at him with her great green eyes, seemingly unconscious of the tears welling up and rolling down her cheeks.

He felt a stab of aching tenderness as he stood up and gathered her in his arms. "Don't cry. Shhhhh! Don't cry," he murmured, patting her like a small child.

"It was so horrible . . . so horrible." He could feel her violent trembling, and drew her closer, his lips against her silken, fragrant hair.

"Shhh! It's all over. Don't cry!" Don't cry, my heart, he said silently, longing to lift her up and carry her to his bed and hold, comfort, and love her the night through. Easy! Easy! he warned himself. She comes to you with her problems, and don't give her more before she's ready for it. He felt her breathing quiet, and she moved out of his arms. He let her go, his perplexing reasons for releasing her were as random-bewildered as his own mind. He'd never felt this tenderness mixed with a consuming desire and he'd certainly never shown this restraint before, and he felt some remnants of resentment. When he found a woman desirable, he never lost an opportunity to follow up any advantage. And this situation, if handled carefully . . . ? So why did he discard such thoughts with a feeling of disgust with himself?

She regarded him steadily. "Thank you, William. I try to shame myself into common sense, but sometimes things get so . . . so *mixed up*, I need someone like you to straighten things out for me!"

He felt a jolt of desire as he looked at her soft, quivering mouth. He wanted to kiss that mouth, kiss it until she begged for mercy. He took a deep breath to steady his voice. "Anytime, Catherine. Come to me anytime! I'll be angry with you if you don't!"

She gave a desolate little laugh. "Sometimes, lately, I feel that I've lost the ability to reason calmly—clearly."

"No," he assured her, putting an arm around her shoulders in a friendly fashion. "You're a gallant young lady with a big heart. But you're quick-tempered, too, and that makes you a little reckless at times! And now . . . off to bed with you. You're ruining your beauty sleep." He longed to hold her, but with a laugh and a little push he sent her on her way, silently, again, protesting his own stupidity.

"I seen w'ere you went!" Tansy exploded grimly when Catherine came through the door. "An' yer don' 'ave to trouble yerself t' say it ain't so!" She was up on one elbow, glaring at her from the truckle bed, her new ruffled nightcap askew, her round eyes rounder. "It's not fitten' fer a young lady . . . not *my* lady!"

Catherine leaned with her back against the door and looked at her friend, all huffed and puffed with indignation like a feisty little hen. She started to laugh ever so softly, and ran over, plopping down on her bed, tailor-fashion, and looked at Tansy with shining eyes.

"Oh, Tansy! He's so wonderful!"

Tansy popped up like a stiff toy on a spring, her face lengthened in shock. "Wonnerful?" she repeated, "*How* . . . wonnerful?"

Catherine let out a whoop of laughter. "Oh, Tansy, you goose! We only *talked!*"

Tansy studied her for a few moments, then let out a sigh of relief.

"Well . . ." she said reluctantly, shaking her head, "I don' know 'ow yer could fin' so much t' talk about!"

Her face sobered. "I was troubled . . . about what I saw today. And I was full of hate. He made me see I was wrong to hate everyone . . . for the actions of some." She made a grimace of disgust. "And I *know* that well enough, Tansy . . . I've *always* known it! But my head doesn't seem to be on quite straight these days! Ever since I left St. Clements, my life has been so different . . . so much more complicated. I've seen some new and awful things, as well as some beautiful things. I guess that life has come at me so fast and furious that my brain just can't take it all in and sort it all out fast enough." She sat still for a while, then sighed deeply and leaned back against the bolsters, smiling again. "Oh, Tansy! I think I'm in love!"

"Could be," she agreed, with a long look at her friend. "But don' jump at 't. Yer on'y gettin' ter know men. An' Mister William 'as been good t' yer. Jus' make sure it ain' jus' feelin' grateful. T'at can trip yer up real fas', an' once yer down fer t' count, yer usually *stays* t'ere an' makes t' bes' of it!"

"Yes." Catherine turned her head on the pillow to look at her. "I'll be sure, Tansy. But"—she drew in a shaky breath—"I don't think gratitude could make me feel all . . . all trembly inside, and make my heart race whenever I look at him. And I think about his kissing me, at the strangest times . . . and I dream . . ." Her voice trailed away and ended in a whisper. "I dream of someday becoming his . . . wife. . . ."

"No," Tansy said, her voice surprisingly serious, "I ain' never 'eard of t'at kind of gratitude!"

CHAPTER SIX

The first day of the festivities for the Coronation of Anne Boleyn dawned with a heavy, milky mist enveloping the Thames, but gradually the sun burned it away and lifted everyone into a holiday mood. The next three days, red and white wine, instead of water, flowed in the fountains and conduits and down the gutters, free to all. There was dancing in the streets, pageants and morality plays, bearbaiting and bullbaiting. The taverns were full to overflowing, and the beggars and pickpockets crowding into the city from near and far had profitable pickings. Even the many, like Catherine, who didn't approve of the new queen, or the circumstances by which she had come to power, were nevertheless willing and excited participants in the festive pageantry.

Catherine's face was glowing with excitement, her eyes sparkled like emeralds. She was seeing, and being a participant in, a thrilling historical event, and she didn't have to fight her way through the crowds or stand on tiptoe to see above them. She was riding like a princess on her uncle's barge, part of the queen's entourage.

Queen Anne Boleyn sat under the canopy of the royal barge, surrounded by a protective ring of the king's guards in their bright halberdiers' uniforms, weapons glinting in the sun. As the barge moved majestically up the Thames, from Greenwich Palace to the Tower of London—bright banners fluttering in the breeze—she now and then lifted a hand or nodded in regal dignity to her subjects, who thronged both sides of the riverbank, waving and cheering over the blare of horns and the sound of tolling bells. From a distance the new queen looked like a pretty French doll with flowing black hair. For six long years she had fought and connived to oust Catherine of Aragon and be crowned queen in her place, and her sparkling dark eyes, which matched the sparkle of jewels on the chaplet encircling her head, seemed to mirror her triumph. She wore a robe of crimson brocade embroidered with pearls, and around a neck that looked too delicate to support her mass of dark hair, she wore a necklace of huge pearls.

Following the royal barge was a concourse of boats lavishly decorated with brilliant-hued banners, streamers, and bunting. First in the line was the state barge of the City of London, carrying the Lord Mayor, clad in scarlet with a heavy gold chain around his neck, and the city dignitaries; then came the boats of the nobility—the peers and peeresses—emblazoned with their colors and coats of arms; the bishops and abbots in red robes, black robes, and white robes; and those of various guilds, their crests and the members' liveries depicting their respective trades. Then came all sizes and shapes of boats—anything that could be paddled—overflowing with shopkeepers and a polyglot of city and country people eager to catch a glimpse of the king and queen and their court.

Music floated from everywhere, and over the din of voices and laughter, delighted "oooohhhhs" and "aaahhhhss" sounded as a writhing and smoking red dragon of Wales, mounted on a barge, sent sprays of flames shooting across the water.

On the second day, the queen was carried through the streets, from the Tower to Westminster Hall, seated beneath a golden canopy in an open litter, hung with cloth of gold and silver. Her dress and surcoat were of softly shimmering silver tissue trimmed in ermine, and she wore a coif of silver with a circlet of rubies on her head. Behind her, in gold carriages draped in red, were her highborn ladies-in-waiting, followed by foot soldiers. As the procession wended its way through the packed streets, the queen occasionally called a halt to watch a lavish allegorical tableau or pageant, always aflutter with white doves—her emblem—or to smile at a group of small children, dressed as choristers, who piped her a musical welcome.

William held Catherine's hand tightly as they mingled with the crowds. They had managed to lose Sheila and Gerald Walker, who had become her persistent suitor, and Catherine felt wickedly happy. They sampled the good Rhenish wine in the fountains, then ate hot, spicy meat pasties and nibbled on sweetmeats while they wandered about watching acrobats and tumblers, archery contests, and wrestling matches. But she was scarcely conscious of anything but William at her side . . . the tingling shock that passed through her each time he took her hand in his . . . the strange breathlessness when their bodies were molded together for a moment in the press of people . . . the irregularity of her heartbeat every time their eyes caught and held in a questing and answering passion. He was going to kiss her, and she was shaken with the desire to feel that beautiful, sensuous mouth on hers.

But he didn't kiss her. Sheila and Gerald found them too soon. William gave her a wry smile and she smiled back, then turned, trying to conceal her aching disappointment. As she turned, she caught an odd expression on Sheila's face. She'd seen that look on her face before. It was the watchful, speculative look of a cat, a cat who knew the mouse it had cornered couldn't possibly escape. A chill shivered across Catherine's skin. For some inexplicable reason she felt threatened by this pretty blonde cousin. She tried to shake off the feeling, telling herself she was being ridiculous, but it remained to plague her the rest of the day.

Whitsunday, June 1, 1533, was sunny and cloudless. Milling crowds, held back by railings, lined the way from Westminster Hall to Westminster Abbey, to view the final procession of Anne Boleyn before she would be officially crowned Queen Anne of England. The long procession entered the Abbey by the West Door, to the blare of trumpets and the swell of triumphant music. Lord and Lady Birchmont and William's distinguished-looking parents, the Duke and Duchess of Chatham, were in the procession, but sons and daughters sat on the rows of marble benches and Catherine and Sheila sat on either side of William. They all stood up as Anne Boleyn walked up the nave on the red carpet, and through the choir stalls on either side, to the shouts of "Vivat Regina Anne! Vivat! Vivat! Vivat!" looking like a tiny regal doll in the cathedral's mammoth-domed immensity, as she was greeted by Thomas Cranmer, Archbishop of Canterbury. Catherine felt a shiver of excitement pass through her as she looked eagerly around, drinking in the scene to store in her memory. It was a picture of magnificence she'd never forget: the brilliant gowns and uniforms, the royal robes of church and state, gleaming swords, golden chains, the sparkle of precious jewels, all set against the solemn marble vastness of Westminster Abbey.

Catherine's eyes slid to William. His handsome face was still thin, all planes and angles, but the convalescent's pallor had disappeared and his cheeks were touched with golden sun. He looked like a tall Nordic king in green velvet embroidered with the gleam of silver—the colors of the House of Chatham—and a flat green velvet hat trimmed with feathers sat on his blond hair. He sat proudly, looking straight ahead, his expression thoughtful. A duke! William will be a duke one day, she thought with a stab of panic. That would make his wife a duchess! Depression settled over her like a shroud. Why would he want *me* for his wife? He could take his pick of beautiful, titled young ladies, with rich dowries. But I *am* of a noble family, she thought with a fierce pride, and William's family is rich and doesn't need a large dowry. So, she admonished herself impatiently, don't be a goose! Your dreams will probably remain just that: dreams! William has never spoken a word of love, or given any sign his intentions are serious. Oh yes, he has that flame of desire in his eyes, but that's a far cry from love, silly goose that you are!

And creeping unbidden into her mind came the same niggling worry about her father. Surely her mother, Lady Anne, would have chosen a man worthy of the name MacRaeggan! But she'd been so young, barely sixteen, and her heart could so easily have ruled over her head, otherwise *why* had it been kept a secret from her family? She found herself wishing fervently that her Uncle Keith would hurry back from the Indies. Maybe he would know. He was the only one alive who had witnessed the heinous scene after the slaughter of the Clan MacRaeggan. Maybe he had discovered his sister's secret. Little, curious boys were known to ferret out the best-kept confidences. Maybe he had the key to unlock the enigma!

William walked with her down to her uncle's barge at the Westminster landing and they had a few minutes alone before the others caught up with them. "I want to see you. I want to be with you, Catherine," he said half angrily, "but it may be impossible for quite some time. I have to return to my home, Fair Meadows. My father has had the management of it all for the past few weeks and he isn't well, as you know."

"I understand," she answered quietly.

"No, you don't!" he snapped. "Oh"—he flung his arm out in a dismissing gesture—"you understand my responsibilities at Fair Meadows, of course . . ." He let out a groan of exasperation. "What you don't understand is that you're driving me out of my mind! I want you! With every breath that's in me, *I want you*. But I've wanted other women and I've had them! You do understand that, don't you, Catherine?" he asked brutally, glaring down at her. He shook her arm. "Answer me!"

Her whole world seemed to be collapsing down around her as she looked at him, her face drained of color. "Yes. I understand that."

"And you don't like it! It disgusts you! Admit it!"

"I have no claim on you, so I have no right to like or dislike it!" Oh, God! Don't cry! she told herself fiercely. Don't you *dare* let him see you cry! "I . . . wouldn't condemn a man, unless," she floundered, "unless he was already married and then . . . had other women . . ."

"Oh, damnation!" he groaned. "Why do you have to be so damn perceptive? I know you think you have feelings for me . . . because you don't know how to hide things like that. But I have to give you time—time to know this life that's new to you. And I have to have time. I think I love you"—he cupped her face gently in his two hands—"but I don't know if it's just because I want you more than I've ever wanted anyone or anything in my life. When I take a wife, it will be *only* because I want to spend the rest of my life with that *one woman*. Perhaps I'm still fighting that final tie." Catherine was trying so desperately to control her need to weep that she couldn't say anything. He sighed explosively. "I want to take you in my arms and hold you and kiss you until you beg for mercy, but your blasted uncle is coming up behind us and I can't . . . *won't* compromise the situation! Catherine," he said hurriedly, "there must be no commitments! No promises! We will both be free to see and do what we please . . . for now. I'll see you when I can. Enjoy yourself, but . . . don't forget me," he murmured softly, looking down into her upturned face.

"I won't," she whispered. "And don't forget me. . . ."

"Never!" His eyes kissed hers, making her weak with longing to feel that kiss on her lips, to feel his strong, hard arms holding her a willing prisoner while they lost themselves in the ecstasy of love. For she loved him with all her wild young heart. . . .

The summer passed in a blaze of heat and humidity that often made sleep impossible for Catherine on those breathless nights that surrendered little of the day's stifling torridness. Time and again she would ease herself out of a damp bed and strip off her nightdress, then stand by the open window and let any little passing breeze cool her perspiration-soaked body. She thought often of the dim, cool stone halls of St. Clements and wondered, with a pull of longing, how her dear Sister Emily fared, and she hoped with all her heart that King Henry would leave the nunnery untouched. Then her thoughts would turn inevitably to William and she would pick apart their last conversation, aching to imbue his words with greater promise, but cautioning herself not to hope for too much.

In spite of the discomfort of the heat she drove herself to restless activity. Every morning after breakfast she tutored Tom and Jack, the Birchmont boys, in Latin, French, and mathematics; they had become close companions, sharing early morning rides along the Thames and through green pastures and nearby woods and along lanes bordered with fields of dark green hops, a second planting of corn and of flax, its bright flowers rippling like a lovely sea of blue.

Immediately after the midday meal she worked in the stillroom, making pomanders of fragrant rose petals, violets, and spices to put among clothing and bed linens. The gardeners' children gathered the roses and brought them to the stillroom in baskets. Tansy often helped, but Sheila preferred to nap or work on her exquisite needle-point, which she could show off to her many admirers. Other times Catherine dried herbs for kitchen and medicinal use, and as she worked, the mouth-watering aroma of cooking fruit wafted in from the kitchen. The cooks were making preserves and syrups from peaches, apples, mulberries, gooseberries, raspberries, and a new fruit, apricot, which she had tasted for the first time and found delicious.

In the afternoons Sheila came alive and—dressed and primped to a fare-thee-well—posed on a garden bench in the shade of a large elm, needlepoint in hand, as she waited the arrival of any young gentlemen callers. And they came, to walk, to talk, to play card and dice games, to challenge the girls at bowling or the game of kayles. And before they departed on any evening, the young men tried to win promises from both girls that they would be their escorts to parties and dances planned after the queen gave birth and the court moved back to London. Catherine enjoyed their company and their attentions, but she put off any promises and was always glad to retire to her room at night to give Tansy lessons in reading and writing, as she had promised, and to reread the letters from William. His father, the duke, was seriously ill and several servants had died of the sweating sickness, so she understood why he hadn't been able to call on her at Birchmont Hall. He always told her he missed her and longed to see her, but he never mentioned "love," which left her frustrated and apprehensive.

It was the last day of August. Catherine had finished her chores, so she changed into a cooler gown and went down to her secret spot on the side of the slope overlooking the Thames. All summer she had watched the boats from here, hoping in vain to see William step ashore. Now she no longer hoped, but just came for a peaceful hour before supper.

"Catherine! Catherine! Where are you? Come quickly!" Sheila's urgent call sent her running up the slope, holding her skirts high, frightening thoughts milling around in her mind.

"What is it, Sheila? What's happened?" she gasped.

Sheila's face was wreathed in smiles as she waved two letters just out of reach. "Guess! Try to guess, Catherine!"

"Oh, please don't tease, Sheila! Tell me!"

"Oh, all right," she agreed at last, her voice full of importance. "Mother just gave these to me. The duke is still ill, so the duchess can't come, but William will be here for your birthday party, September third." Catherine's heart was hammering so hard, she didn't hear the rest of what Sheila was saying. I'm going to see William! At last! At last! she told herself as an anticipatory shiver ran through her. Sheila observed her closely with that same watchful, speculative look as she held out the second piece of paper. "The second surprise, Catherine. Your *brother* is coming home . . ."

"My *brother*? Oh! Oh, my brother *Keith!*" How could you forget? she groaned silently. Just the mention of William's name paralyzes your mind! *Your Uncle Keith is supposed to be your brother!* "How wonderful! When?"

A ghost of a smirk was on Sheila's face as she glanced down at the letter. "He will arrive in London the ninth of September, if all goes well. His wife, Cecily, is not well and he hopes the good physicians of London will be able to bring her to good health. Aren't you excited, Catherine?"

"Oh yes! Yes! I've so wanted to see my brother!"

"And *William*," Sheila finished for her in a dry voice.

"Yes . . . *and William!*" Catherine said, looking at her defiantly.

Abruptly Sheila was again all smiles, and she grasped Catherine's arm in a sisterly fashion as they hurried to the house, chattering about the many guests who were coming and what gowns they would wear. Catherine was laughing as she burst into her room. Tansy was putting freshly ironed gowns into the clothespress.

"Tansy! Guess what? My Uncle Keith is coming home, and William will be here for my birthday party!"

"Oh, Miss Catherine! That's wonderful news!" They looked at each other with glowing eyes, then with shrieks of happy laughter they grabbed arms and danced around the room, finally collapsing on Catherine's bed, too out of breath to talk.

Catherine leaned forward. The ravishing girl in the mirror did the same. She studied her curiously, as if she were regarding a stranger. The soft, grass-green velvet gown made her eyes green sapphires, and the new farthingale held her skirts out fashionably full and made her waist small enough to be spanned by a man's two hands. A design in silver metallic thread outlined the square neckline and blended into the soft white skin above her swelling breasts. Her eyes moved over the silken sheen of her black hair, the excited color staining her cheeks and her lips as luscious and pink as ripe strawberries. She didn't feel like the Catherine who had known only the scratch of rough homespun for her first sixteen years.

"Oh, Tansy! I didn't know so much happiness could fit into one body!"

"He'll ask you tonight! I knows he will! I saw t' look on 'is face!"

"Oh, I hope and pray so! If I have to wait any longer I'll burst!"

She paused and looked down the staircase at the beautifully clad guests milling around in the Great Hall. They were friends of the elder Birchmonts and many younger friends of hers and Sheila's from surrounding estates. She spotted Sir Howard and his wife and sons Gerald and Boyd talking to pretty young ladies, and the great Sir Thomas More, who lived near them here, in Chelsea. The two huge brass chandeliers, held in position by pulleys, were ablaze with candles, and under the lights jewels glittered among the softer glow of golden chains and the hilts of fancy swords.

As she started down, William appeared at the bottom step, looking up at her. She faltered and caught the balustrade for an almost imperceptible moment, released it, and continued to descend, step by step, as if moving in a dream. She was so achingly conscious only of him that everyone and everything else faded into nothingness. He was in the same green and silver outfit he'd worn at the Coronation and, inadvertently, they were a handsomely matched pair. He stared at her with savage intensity. She managed a tremulous smile, but he didn't smile back. His eyes slowly searched her face, caressing it, as if he wanted to imprint her loveliness on his mind forever. Then his eyes rested on her lips and, as always, she felt them quiver under his silent kisses. Finally his eyes looked into hers, burning into her very soul. She was powerless to look away, and they stared at each other breathlessly, in the wondrous stillness of the pain-and-joy-filled discovery and promise of mutual love.

"Happy birthday, my love . . . my dearest love," he whispered as he raised her hand to his lips, searing his mark into her flesh.

"Thank you, William, my love," she murmured as a fierce, joyful trembling rose within her.

"I must talk to you, darling. Alone," he whispered. "Meet me at the stables in the morning . . . seven o'clock. I'll have the horses ready for a ride. Then . . . at a special place . . . a *special question* . . ."

She looked up into his face, her green eyes shining with all the intensity of her love, longing to fling her arms around his neck. "Oh, William, dearest, I'll be there!" she breathed as the dancing commenced, giving them no more opportunity for private conversation.

The evening passed in a haze of happiness for Catherine, and her glowing beauty bewitched everyone around her. She was touched and overwhelmed by the thoughtful, lovely presents and the grand, painstakingly planned dinner. An immense cake, aflame with candles, was brought in, followed by a procession of minstrels, who sang her a birthday wish and a riddle. She cut the ring cake and discovered the ring in her piece, which brought cheers, and sly glances at William, as if they knew their secret. As they all got up, glasses raised in a toast, Catherine was aware, for a brief instant, of the look of open consternation on the faces of her aunt and uncle and the expression of pure venom in Sheila's eyes. What makes me feel like this: uneasy, half fearful? she thought, As if I'm always *waiting* for something terrible to happen! As if there is something evil hanging over my head, threatening me . . . something suspended by a thread that's too weak to hold the weight of it . . . for too long!

Without a word he held out his arms and Catherine flew to him with a low cry of happiness. He grunted softly as he caught the full weight of her body, then he crushed her close, smothering her face and her hair with kisses. His shirt was open at the neck and her cheek was against the smooth silken hair on his broad chest.

"Catherine . . . my darling . . . my love!" he cried fiercely. "I've been going out of my mind these months trying not to love you . . . trying to tell myself I didn't want you, but"—he gave a helpless laugh—"my mind told me I lied! I knew all the time I couldn't live without your love!" He nuzzled and nibbled at her ears and powdered her with a gentle shower of kisses that changed into flaming, urgent demands, and she felt herself changing into a passionate wanton. She clung to him, fitting her slim, soft body to his in wild abandonment, feeling the sensuous thrill of his hard, urgent maleness. His searching lips burned into hers with bruising madness, then moved slowly downward over her throat and found the firm warmth of her breasts. His burning kisses and his sure muscular hands that caressed her so gently were drugging her senses, carrying her to dizzying heights of passion beyond her wildest dreams. She was enveloped in a dreamy acquiescence which left her totally responsive to his passionate demands.

"I love you, William! I . . . love . . . you so!" she murmured breathlessly. "I've been so . . . afraid!"

He held her away from him for a moment, looking deep into her eyes. "Don't ever be afraid again, my heart. I love only you. I want only you." He closed his eyes with a groan as he tightened his arms around her.

With a deep reluctant breath he took her arms from about his neck. He slowly kissed each fingertip, then held them prisoner. "If I don't take care, I'll forget myself." He nuzzled her hair, delighting in the soft silken fragrance of her, then kissed her softly and put her aside. "Now!" He gestured toward the shorter of the two saddled horses, standing patiently at the stable entrance.

"Her name is Lady Dileas, Scottish for 'beloved,' and she's yours."

"Mine! Oh, William! Oh, darling! She's beautiful!" Catherine looked at him with glowing eyes, then rubbed her cheek against the velvety nose of the Welsh cob, crooning to her softly, "Lady Dileas . . . Dileas . . . beloved. You named her rightly, William. It suits her." She stepped back and admired the strong, powerful body, the shine of her chestnut coat, the small proud head with white markings.

"My birthday present to you, dearest one."

"How can I thank you enough?" Her eyes adored him.

"Love me. Love me, Catherine," he commanded in a whisper.

"I do, my heart, I do."

The morning air felt fresh and invigorating with its nip of fall as they rode at an easy canter past yellow silken fields that flowed up to the edge of the bosky woods, where here and there a slender dark evergreen was silhouetted like an exclamation point against the thin blue of the sky. They tethered their horses, and William held her hand tightly as he guided her along a narrow footpath etched faintly in dark brown earth against the fecund green floor. Abruptly there was a clearing, and Catherine caught her breath, unable to speak.

"My own private chapel. I feel close to God here, Catherine. Away from the rich trappings of church and state."

"I understand," she said softly. "It's a place of God-made beauty. A place of magic, of peace." Her eyes drank in the beauty all around her. A crystal waterfall splashed down into a lovely clear pool, sending circular ripples into the mint massing the water's edge in fresh, piquant fragrance, then overflowed into a slow-moving stream that gurgled and bubbled as it meandered through the green frondy place and disappeared. Overhead the trees touched one another with delicate leafy fingers, covering them with a lacy green canopy, alive with sweet birdsong. There were carpets of fern and wildflowers: monkshood, with its deeply cut leaves and showy hooded flowers in yellow here, purple there, and white there at the base of hairy old trees; and there was bittersweet, fall fruiting with its scarlet berries. How could two plants be so beautiful and yet so poisonous? Catherine thought as she regarded them in silent wonder.

William drew her down on the grass alongside the pool and they looked down at their smiling reflections that wavered and changed with the ripples. He turned her to face him and they looked long at each other, eyes solemn, fingers touching. "Catherine, I love you with all of my heart and soul. Will you do me the great honor of becoming my wife?"

"Yes, William, I will." Her voice trembled, but her wide green eyes regarded him steadily. "For I love you with every breath that's in me."

He took a ring from the pocket of his leather jerkin and placed it on the ring finger of her left hand. The large ruby glowed like fire in a thin ray of sunshine that knifed its way through the leafy canopy, and the encircling pearls were handsomely matched.

Catherine looked from the ring to William, with her heart in her eyes, and she thought, I wish I could catch and hold this moment in a transparent bubble of precious gold, safe from the erosion of time! I could hold it in my hands and look at it—whenever I wished—and relive the heart-stopping beauty of this moment, when we promised to love each other forever.

"It's an exquisite ring. I'll treasure it always."

"It was my great-grandmother's betrothal ring, then my grandmother's and my mother's. He looked long into her sweet and lovely face. "How I love you, Mistress Catherine Birchmont!" A stab of fear went through her. Now is the time. I must *tell* him, she thought despairingly. "You'll have to wear the ring on the chain of your necklace until your brother Keith returns." He felt her stiffen as he took her gently in his arms. "Don't look so serious, my sweet. I spoke to Lord Birchmont last night and he says we must have your brother Keith's permission. Keith is your true next of kin and the head of your family." He ruffled her hair in teasing tenderness. "Don't worry. He'll grant permission without a doubt. Heaven knows Lady Birchmont has tried every trick in the book to marry me off to Sheila!" he laughed. "So at least I have chosen *one* of the Birchmonts!" His powerful arms held her captive, and helplessly she lifted her lips to meet his kiss with a hunger that matched his own, until there were only two of them peopling their own glorious world.

Finally, reluctantly, she moved away from his intoxicating arms and lips, smoothing the skirts of her riding costume in a semicircle on the ground around her, face downcast, trying to marshal her thoughts so she could tell him in a calm, coherent manner. It was no use, she decided hopelessly. There was no way to cushion such a shock . . . "William—I'm not a Birchmont!" she blurted. "I'm only slightly related through my great-grandmother!"

He looked at her with a grin. "I surmised that some time ago, little one. You were raised by the nuns at St. Clements, not *raised* by a relative in York and *educated* by the nuns!"

"How . . . how did you know?"

He kissed her lightly on either cheek, then took her hands and turned them palms up. "Your hands are soft and white now. They were calloused from hard work." He planted a kiss in each one. "You were unused to rich, plentiful food, and you have no rigid class-consciousness or stultifying coyness of the Tudor ladies, thank God! And," he continued more soberly, "you cried out bitterly against the *part* of you that's English when you saw the two Scotsmen who'd been killed, so I assumed you are more Scot than English. And what difference does it make?"

She tried to say, "I don't know who my father is!" but she couldn't bring the words past her lips. She had another few days of grace before he might find this out from Keith, and she was suddenly afraid to spoil this day of the greatest happiness she'd ever known. After all, what difference could a few days make?

"How transparent I must have been," she said finally with a laugh.

"No." He shook his head. "Only to me, perhaps, because I was watching you with very critical eyes, trying to find faults. I wasn't ready to fall in love."

She got quickly to her feet. "Are you *certain*, William, that you're ready to give up . . ." She couldn't finish the thought, but the meaning was clear. "I—I must tell you this, William"—she swallowed hard—"that if you ever took another woman after we were married, I would leave your house no matter how my heart was breaking!"

"You can't leave your husband's house," he baited her coolly. "A husband *owns* his wife . . . like a horse . . . or a piece of furniture! He's even allowed to beat her, if he wishes and she deserves it, for displeasing him!"

She almost choked in her angry frustration. "I'm trying to be honest! Trying to explain my deepest feelings, and you seem to find it amusing!"

"Because you're talking nonsense!" His fingers bit into her arms. "Do you think I could ever violate your love by taking another woman?" he demanded fiercely. Catherine didn't trust herself to speak, afraid the words would gush out on tears of relief. His voice grew husky with emotion. "When I hold a woman in my arms like this"—he molded her to him as if they were one—"and make love to her . . . when I long with every beat of my heart to be with her and I'm miserable every moment away from her . . . when I want to father her children—many, many of them"—he nuzzled the warm hollow of her neck—"then I've given my heart forever! Then I'm *in love* for the first time and there's no room in my heart for anyone else!" With a firm but gentle hand he lifted her face to his. "I give you my heart, Catherine." His lips drew the very breath out of her, and she gave herself up to the flood of desire pulsing through her. "How I'm going to keep you innocent and untouched until our marriage night is beyond me!" he groaned, releasing her. Then he ticked the tip of her nose teasingly. "And, lovely miss, I plan to keep you constantly with child!" They were still for a moment, caught in a hypnotic spell. To break the spell he caught her hand, and they ran through the woods to their horses, stopping once to embrace in sheer delight at the wonder of their love and the beauty of the world that seemed to stretch, untroubled and sunny, before them . . . too blind to realize that there is usually a lull before a storm. . . .

"Whatever are we going to do? *You* tell me!" Lady Birchmont demanded in icy fury as she paced up and down in the bedroom later that night. She stopped to glare at her husband, who leaned against the mantel, disheveled and tight-lipped. "It's gone too far! Can you *imagine* what this will do to us *socially*—even *financially* —if the truth about Catherine gets out? Oh!" She shook her raised fists toward heaven in an agony of frustration. "Why did you ever bring her to London? You must tell her now!"

He groaned aloud and slumped down on a bench, running his hands through his hair until it stood on end like a bristling, graying porcupine. "It will destroy her!" he shouted, his face purpling.

"Shhhh! Keep your voice down!" she hissed. "Do you want to

wake up the whole house? And what do you think it will do to us? It could destroy Sheila's chances of a good marriage . . . even the boys' chances!" She grabbed a stool and dragged it close to him, pinning him down with her desperate eyes. "I had no idea how serious William was. He didn't call all summer. I thought it was just a passing fancy. He wrote to her, yes. But just silly claptrap. No mention of love."

He looked at her with a frown. "How do you know that?"

She ignored the question. "She's not a child. She has to know sometime, and the quicker the better."

He gave her a long, level appraisal. "No, she's not a child, but I want her to have a little more time . . . to give her strength . . . to give her courage."

"Did you tell William that Keith's arrival has been postponed for a few weeks?"

"No." He shook his head. "I was afraid he might insist on *my* permission. William has always observed the social rules, but he's a stubborn young man, who has an uncanny way of surmounting obstacles that appear insurmountable to others. I'll tell Catherine and persuade her to write him to be patient."

At her uncle's urging, Catherine wrote and pleaded patience, then wrote again when there was another postponement because Keith's wife was too weak to tolerate the long sea voyage. Then the Duke of Chatham suffered another seizure and was completely paralyzed, so William had to stay at his father's side during the first crucial period. Winter was settling over England, with its cold, deep fogs and sleet storms that iced windows and cracked fingers open with chilblains. The weeks of waiting had taken their toll of Catherine. She was thinner and more withdrawn as she went about her daily routine, and she missed the young Birchmont boys, who wouldn't be home until the Christmas holidays. They were confined to the house for days when the roads were bad or the fogs made it impossible to travel on the Thames. The weather also dictated the flow of visitors, mostly young men, and kept parties to a minimum, which didn't bother Catherine. It only bothered her that the mail was always so late. She lived for William's letters and his impassioned words of love, and his promises that they would be together soon whether they had Keith's permission or not. She read them until the paper became too worn to handle, but they were a poor substitute for seeing him and holding him, as she longed to do.

Sheila and Lady Birchmont were often bored and out-of-sorts, and they seemed to take their irritation out on Catherine, so she was always glad to hurry up to her room and bask in Tansy's comforting, happy chatter. Tansy and Frank were getting married at the turn of the new year, and the two girls sewed every possible evening on things for Tansy's small dowry. Usually she kept a check on her troubled thoughts, but once in a while she had to unburden herself.

"Everything seems to have gone wrong since I became a part of the Birchmont family, Tansy! Almost as if I were a . . . a . . . *disturbing force.*" She spread her hands out in a helpless gesture. "I took William from Sheila . . ."

"How could y'r take him from 'er? She never had 'im in t' first place!"

"Well, she's unhappy, bitter, and she can't seem to settle on anyone else."

"A pox on 'er fer her sharp tongue! Maybe no one else wants her!"

"And everything seems to be happening . . . *conspiring* to keep William and me apart: the weather, the roads, illness, Uncle Keith! Oh, Tansy! Where is it going to end? It frightens me! Sometimes I feel as if some strange, dark strategies are being played around me, but my face is to the wall and I can't *see them.* I can only *sense them!*"

Tansy said no more. She had been brought up on omens and portents, good signs and bad, and while she didn't believe some, she was afraid to ridicule others, which might be tempting fate. . . .

The bitter cold was finally gentled by a warmer current washing the English shores, giving them a respite from winter's icy grip. Skies were clear and blue, the Thames exploded with boats and barges, and bright fluttering sails, and hundreds of swans came out from their reedy hideaways and sailed with the river's meander, majestically unruffled by the heavy traffic. As if blossoming under the sun's beneficence, callers came, in sufficient numbers to please even Sheila. Invitations to parties arrived, and with them, several letters from William, the latest stating he would be at Birchmont Hall on the 15th of December—some twenty days hence—and he would make their plans known to Lord Birchmont, and to Keith, if he were there, and to the king. But, permission or no, their betrothal would be announced. To the king! Oh no! Catherine's stomach tied in a hurting knot. The king would never grant a marriage of the son of the Duke of Chatham to a girl of unknown lineage on her father's side! On the heels of William's letter came an invitation from King Henry VIII and Queen Anne to a ball at Whitehall Palace, and the next few days passed in a dither of preparation.

As the wherry boat was nosed into place at the Whitehall Palace landing, Catherine was filled with a feverish excitement that momentarily pushed the worries and fears of the past few days into the back of her mind. When the king and his court were in residence, it somehow created a feeling of magical glitter—the pulse and pace of the city increased and touched the surrounding areas with a special feeling of importance. She had so wanted to visit Whitehall, but her uncle always found some reason not to. It was much more a public palace than other palaces of the royal family. The public, if suitably dressed, was allowed to attend outdoor sermons in the Sermon Court, or to walk in the gardens and to watch the king and court at games in the tilting yard or on the tennis courts.

Liveried servants leaped to help the Birchmonts out of the boat, and as they ascended the Privy Stairs, west of the public Whitehall Stairs, their way was lighted all the way up to the Stone Gallery by huge flaming torches held by a line of some two dozen men. Music and laughing chatter floated around them as they walked through the Stone Gallery and entered the Privy Gallery that joined it to the east. The ballroom sparkled and glittered like a great golden cavern, hung with cloths of gold and silver and lighted with thousands of candles. Emblazoned everywhere were the king's arms under crowns imperial, supported by richly painted royal beasts, and the noise of merrymaking pulsed counterpoint to the strains of the music. It was like stepping into a fairy tale world of jewels and lights and brilliant dress.

"Oh, Uncle John, isn't it magnificent? It looks just like I dreamed it would!" Catherine's eyes shone, her face was colored with excitement.

He smiled and squeezed her hand. "It's quite a pageant," he commented dryly, "but I'm happy you're pleased." She wasn't aware of his scrutiny and had no thought at the moment of how utterly lovely she was in her gown of cream velvet with its cream and gold brocade underskirt, belted with a girdle of gold, and her midnight-black hair caught in a golden caul.

Sheila and Catherine were surrounded almost immediately by admirers and carried off to dance. The dancing, the warmth of the press of bodies, the wine and the heady compliments had a soporific effect on Catherine, and she felt as if she were floating in a rose-filled dream, a pleasant change from the nightmares she'd been having of late. Abruptly the music stopped and heralds in scarlet and gold trumpeted the arrival of the king and queen, and Lord Birchmont quickly guided his three ladies into one of the two lines that formed an aisle to the throne chairs set up on a dais.

Catherine studied the royal couple eagerly as they came toward her. The king was tall, nearly six feet, three inches, corpulent, and looked enormous in a padded and slashed doublet of yellow velvet that ended just above his knees, embroidered in silver and gold and belted with gold chains. He wore a round-sleeved overjacket of scarlet velvet collared in ermine, yellow silk hose, scarlet leather square-toed shoes, slashed and puffed with yellow silk, a white linen shirt, its slashed sleeves caught together with jeweled buttons, and his prominent codpiece was heavily embroidered. A flat yellow velvet hat with a large white plume sat on his auburn hair; the chain about his neck was studded with magnificent gems and from it hung the jeweled pendant of St. George, and his fingers were loaded with rings of precious stones. He looked like a moving mountain of brilliant glitter.

Catherine had expected a more queenly figure of a woman, with greater presence, beauty, and grace; then she could have better understood how the king was so enamored he suffered excommunication from the Catholic Church and risked his subjects' displeasure by taking such a woman to be their queen. Anne Boleyn was small-bosomed, with a long, thin neck, masses of dark hair, a swarthy complexion, and black sloe-eyes. She was dressed like a queen, however, in a gold-tissue gown, embroidered with pearls and cuffed in ermine. A gold gable headdress framed her face; she wore a necklace of huge pearls and many glittering rings, cleverly concealing the deformity on her left hand—a growth that looked like the beginning of a sixth finger—against the folds of her gown as she walked.

As they drew abreast of the Birchmont party, Catherine was sharply aware of the arrested turn of the king's head and the focusing of his hypnotic gaze on her. She executed a graceful curtsy, then felt her hand swallowed in his as he drew her upright to face him, and she heard Lord Birchmont presenting her to the royal couple.

"I am greatly honored, Your Majesty." She curtsied again, then looked up at him. His blue eyes, sunken into pockets of fat, studied her with a proprietary gleam of admiration.

"Ah! The lovely Mistress Birchmont! Your beauty was exaggerated not one whit, my dear! You are like a beautiful and rare precious gem!"

The years had coarsened and bloated him. No longer was he the "Golden Prince," or "the handsomest prince in Christendom," as she had heard all her growing-up years. His hair was still auburn, his eyes still blue, but his nose . . . ! Catherine had seen a painting showing him full face, and was not prepared for the high-bridged, massive protuberance in profile.

"Thank you, Your Majesty." She dipped and slightly inclined her head, very conscious of the queen, who was conversing vivaciously with Lord Birchmont. But the lines were hard around the queen's pasted-on smile and her eyes were watchful.

"You must have a dance with me, Mistress Catherine," he said as he moved on along the line.

"Thank you, Your Majesty." She curtsied again, feeling as if her head would bob off. For the rest of the evening she was the center of all eyes. The king had paid her open tribute, quite different from his usual teasing, flirtatious manner with pretty young ladies of the court at festive celebrations, and everyone was watching for his next move. He was bursting with unctuous good humor as he led his gay and vivacious queen and other ladies in spirited dance, and he performed, after some persuasion, remarkably well on the lute, singing a light love lyric he had composed. But later he moved directly toward Catherine in a straight line—as his courtiers opened a path—drawn as a magnet moves toward an irresistible object, and claimed his dance, which extended into the usual four of the suite.

For all his corpulence and his ulcerous leg, he was light and graceful, and pleasant and intelligent in his conversation. The dramatic timbre of his voice matched the majestic size of him and imbued his words with emphatic power, so everything he said could be heard by all those nearby. But his conversation was beyond reproach as he discussed music and art—his two greatest cultural interests—and his additional plans for Whitehall Palace and Hampton Court, the second elegant estate he had wrested from Cardinal Wolsey. Catherine had no difficulty discoursing with him because she felt no particular reverence for his person, nor was she awestruck in his presence. He was delighted with her wit and intelligence as they spoke in French and Latin, and he so expressed himself at times with an almost boyish candor and a smile of great charm. Unaccountably, she felt drawn to this man and, to her surprise, she felt herself smiling in return. It was said he could charm his worst enemy with his smile, if he chose. He used this powerful charm like a deliberate talent, and since she didn't really trust or like him, she had to fight consciously against it.

"You must come often to court," he commanded as he surrendered her to Lord Birchmont. "I insist on it. Perhaps the queen could do with another lady-in-waiting."

Catching the lustful look in his eyes again, she felt a sense of embarrassment, as if she had read his private thoughts. "It would be an honor, Your Majesty," she said, hoping her words sounded convincing.

A silent scream rose within her as she watched him walk back to his queen, followed by several courtiers, who had been waiting at a respectful distance until he concluded his conversation. She felt as if a net were being drawn around her, rendering her more and more helpless to follow her own wishes. She didn't want any part of the king or his queen. She had seen that look often enough in men's eyes and she knew it meant nothing but trouble. The queen was no fool. She had schemed and clawed her way to the highest position in the land and she would not tolerate another woman around in whom her husband had evinced interest, fearful the woman would supplant her, as she had supplanted Catherine of Aragon. Catherine had wanted to tell the king that she would be taking a husband after the new year, but again, she had no right to discuss it until the betrothal was announced, and again, she thought with a sick falling-away feeling in the pit of her stomach, perhaps it would never come to pass. . . .

The dancing ended in a sumptuous banquet, then most of the guests joined the royal couple in the gambling game of mumchance, so Lord Birchmont offered to show Catherine around the palace. When they reached the library, he took her hand in his. "Catherine," he began reluctantly, I'm afraid I have some bad news. I was in the company of Thomas Cromwell this evening, and overheard his remark that St. Clements is to be torn down . . . destroyed."

"St. Clements!" she gasped. Why? It's a small, poor nunnery. Only a few precious relics! The king could take *those!* Why does he have to tear it down and turn out the nuns?"

"It's because it's small and rather poor! The land and materials are worth more in money . . . in favors . . . than a few pious nuns!"

"I'll go to the king! Plead with him to spare it!"

"You'll do nothing of the sort!" he said, aghast. "No one interferes with the king's—or Cromwell's—plans for the monastic houses! Influential men have tried and . . ." He moved his finger across his throat.

She stared at him stonily, but finally her shoulders sagged

despondently. "You're right, of course, Uncle John. It's futile! The king is so ruthless in his greed! I'd only cause trouble for everyone in the family. I must go to Sister Emily." Her voice firmed with resolve. "She will be confused—lost. She's old, Uncle John, and she'll have nowhere to go."

"Nonsense!" His mouth was a grim line. "What can a slip of a girl do? The day following Christmas, I'll send two or three of my men to bring her back to London."

"I'll go with them!" As she opened her mouth to continue, he closed it with a gentle hand.

"No, and that's the end of that!"

She felt a cold panic coiling within her. She knew Sister Emily. She would fight to the last breath for her convictions and she'd never desert her sisters in their time of trouble. I'll have to go or she'll stay until the last stone of St. Clements is struck down around her, and maybe . . . she thought with a shiver . . . her head along with it!

They returned late from the ball and Sheila hurried up to her room, still seething with resentment, which she took out on her maid. The poor girl finally burst into tears and Sheila screeched at her to get out and threw a hairbrush at her to hurry her on the way. "I hate Catherine!" she whispered to the blonde girl in the mirror. "Hate her! She casts her spell over everyone: my father . . . William . . . and now the king!" She punctuated every name with a pounding of her fist on the cupboard. Her sullen brown eyes darkened with secretive, ugly thoughts and a smile touched her lips. "Now!" she whispered exultantly. "Now is the time to tell Catherine! Now, before William comes and before the king becomes so enamored with her that he has to be told . . . to the shame of the entire Birchmont family!" She quickly changed into a night-robe, then tiptoed down the hall and tapped on Catherine's door.

"I want to talk to you, Catherine . . ."

Catherine groaned inwardly. She was bone-weary and worried sick about Sister Emily and she didn't relish a conversation with Sheila, which was usually unpleasant, and she wished Tansy were there instead of somewhere with Frank. "Very well, Sheila, come in.

She glanced sharply at the girl as she settled on a bench before the dying fire. Sheila seemed caught in the grip of some inexplicable excitement that made her a little breathy and put two spots of color high in her cheeks. Catherine lighted two candles, then sat down and waited.

"I know who fathered you."

"What?"

"I said, I know who your father is!" Her voice was high and unsteady.

Catherine heard the heavy drumming of blood in her ears as she stared at the young blonde girl with stunned intensity. Was this a terrible jest? She wouldn't put it past her! Fear breeds caution, and Catherine asked cautiously, "How would you know something that my . . . my brother and my uncle don't?"

"Ha!" she snorted. "Your brother! Keith is your uncle, the brother of Lady Anne MacRaeggan . . . your mother! And they do know who your father is; they are just too cowardly to tell you! But . . . I'm not . . . I'll tell you!" she said in insidious softness. Her sardonic smile held secret, malicious amusement.

Catherine got to her feet, shaking as if in the throes of a hard chill. She wanted to move toward the girl, but a heavy sense of calamity rooted her to the floor. "Then . . . then . . . tell me!" she whispered hoarsely.

"Your mother was captured and taken to Castle MacOrvan after the slaughter of the Clan MacRaeggan." Her voice scarcely scratched the suffocating silence. "There she was violated by Graham MacOrvan, idiot son of Sir James MacOrvan! Did you hear me, Catherine? Your father is an idiot who is kept locked up in the castle's tower! He was brought to your mother by guards, with a chain around his neck!

Sheila's face was ravaged by hatred. "Do you understand, Catherine? You were fathered by an idiot!" Peal after peal of her mocking laughter rang out. "You can never marry! If you had children they would be idiots!" Even as she said the words they sounded unreal, grotesque.

A corner of Catherine's mind opened a crack. "No!" Her thin cry hung in the air, then dissolved into a dry strangled sob of denial: "No! No!"

Sheila watched her with a look of bright malevolence, but her expression changed to alarm as Catherine exploded in piercing, unearthly screams that reached every corner of the house. She frantically tried to quiet her, but to no avail, and Catherine turned on her with a pathetically instinctive reaction, beating on her as the bearer of tragic news. "It's not true! You lie! You lie!" she shrieked over and over.

The door burst open, and Lord Birchmont and Tansy charged in, falling over each other in their anxiety, and quickly separated the two. Lord Birchmont looked from one girl's face to the other, marking the triumphant malice in the face of his daughter and the deathlike shock on Catherine's, which could mean only one thing. "What have you done, Sheila? What have you told her?" he demanded.

"I told her about her father, Graham MacOrvan," she said with a defiant shrug, as her father looked at her as if she had just committed murder.

A look of sick helplessness passed over Lord Birchmont's face, and the horror and agony of its truth crystallized in Catherine's innermost depths. She drew in a breath and let out a shuddering moan, as she fell into a deep abyss of unconsciousness.

Time and again she awoke sweating and terrified from her drug-induced dreams, to feel the comforting hand of Tansy smoothing her hair back from her forehead or talking to her in low soothing tones. Like an obedient child she took the medicine they gave her. Tortured dreams were preferable to ghastly reality. On the second day she awoke, blinking her eyes against the sunlight streaming through her window.

"Tansy?" she murmured weakly. No one answered, and she was suddenly overwhelmed with panic. The room swam about her in a sickening haze as she tried to force loathsome reality away into the back of her mind, as one does with things difficult to explain and impossible to accept. She had always been able to face things and make decisions, but now she wasn't dealing with tangibles. There was nothing she could reach out and grasp with her hands and change by her own physical effort. This was like a shapeless, insidiously poisonous fog that enveloped her in a suffocating shroud, penetrating her mind, immobilizing her with terror, smothering her will to fight, to claw it away so she could think or reason with any clarity.

What have I done to deserve such punishment? What did my mother ever do, or the whole Clan MacRaeggan? Her tormented spirit wandered, pouncing on hidden thoughts, dragging them out into the mercilous light of conscious reality, stunning her by the brutal picture-clarity of her mother suffering and of the bloody bodies of her clansmen scattered through Gullhaven, murdered on the strength of a fiendish *lie!* And . . . *William!* The pain at the thought of him was as if her heart were being torn in two. They could never marry! She could never bear children! What was it he had said? He would keep her always with child! She gave a bark of laughter that scalded her throat with its bitterness. She lay there, eyes dry, heart and mind benumbed, her pain and sorrow beyond the relief of tears. *All that I will ever have of love is what I carry in my memory, and it will have to last me all the dreary years of my lifetime!*

Excruciatingly slow, her anguish gave way to rational thought. She would have to leave Birchmont Hall immediately. She would go to York, to St. Clements, and find a place of comfort and safety for Sister Emily. And then her mouth twisted in a tortured grimace as she whispered, "There is no use tormenting myself. I can never undo the hideous events of the past. What's done is done. I am the daughter of an idiot!" Bitter gorge rose in her throat and she was convulsed with uncontrollable shudders. "But," she vowed in a choking whisper, "I will seek out Sir James MacOrvan and avenge my family!"

Travel on the Great North Road was difficult enough in the pleasant months but so incredibly bad in the winter that the villagers usually just holed up, waiting until a warming spell allowed them a trip to market or the alehouse. Catherine had no choice than to press on for day after dreary day, through the nightmare of ice and shrieking winds, of roads so mucky or frozen she often had to keep Dileas at a snail's pace. Several times her swift, surefooted mare left pursuing highwaymen far behind and carried her on to the safety of a poor alehouse or a farmer's barn, where she slept snuggled into a pile of fragrant hay.

As if regretting its violent severity, the weather capriciously welcomed her to York with its gentler side, and the town surged with renewed vigor. Water from melting ice ran swiftly down the center gutters, pushing the garbage away before the rooting pigs could gobble it up; ducks waddled around the marketplace, snitching produce; animal deposits steamed in the sun; outside stalls were doing a brisk business as buyers fingered the wares and bargained vigorously. Fishmongers called out the succulent delight of "melwell and mackerel" above the rattle and clatter of horses and carts, and over it all was the incessant ringing of bells.

"There it is, Dileas . . . St. Clements!" she murmured as she caught sight of the gray stone cluster of arches and spires, the windows turned to gold in the afternoon sun, just as she remembered. She felt the tears lump in her throat. "We'll go around the back." She looped the reins over the wooden hooks and tried the gate. It was locked, so she pulled on the bell: once, twice, and a third time, which brought the sound of a voice grumbling:

"Yes! Yes! Keep ye now! You don't have to ring it off!" Sister Emily looked the young man up and down. At least he wasn't a beggar! she thought with a sigh. There was little enough to share these days! "Yes? What is it you wish, young man?"

With a tremulous laugh Catherine swept off her hat with its bedraggled plume and her hair fell down around her shoulders in a shimmering mass. Don't you recognize me, Sister Emily?"

Her mouth was a soundless "O" in her wrinkled face as she clapped her hands and cried, "Catherine! Oh, my child! My child! I thought I would never set eyes on you again! Oh, thank God for His kindness!" They laughed and cried through their hugs and tears, and finally, arm in arm, they went in search of the Abbess.

It was dark when Catherine walked with the sisters in candlelit procession to the chapel for Compline, the last liturgical prayer of the day. It was cold, and she drew her fur-lined cloak around her heavy velvet dress as she kneeled down on the hard bench and looked around at the hooded heads reverently bowed, at the beautiful altar lighted by candles and agleam with gold and silver and richly colored cloths. The same lovely colors were in the magnificent stained glass windows on either side of the chapel. She looked, but felt nothing but a terrible emptiness. As the musical rise and fall of the priest's voice came to an end, she buried her face in her hands and tried to pray. She found it hard these days, and when she did pray, her inner pleadings to God were those of a frightened human soul: Don't let it be true; wake me up from this nightmare, please, God! But He didn't hear or heed her.

The sisters retired to their beds after the service, but the Abbess and Catherine talked long into the night.

"You haven't been deserted, my child," she remonstrated earnestly. "God performs His wonders in many ways mysterious to us—"

"Yes, I know all that, Reverend Mother," she broke in bitterly. "But why me? Oh!" She gave a sigh of resignation. "We've gone over all this, and I realize, as you say, that there are many thousands, less fortunate than I who ask God the same question: 'Why me?'"

"I will pray for your peace of mind, Catherine. And you must not live in constant fear that the same madness will come upon you. I know it will not!"

"How can you be so sure? The thought haunts me day and night!" Her tormented cry throbbed in the air between them.

The Abbess took her cold, slim hands in her old ones, roughened by spartan living. "Look at me, my child." Never had Catherine seen such an expression of deep inner peace. Whatever trials the Abbess had been burdened with, she had accepted and conquered. "Believe me, and keep faith with God!"

"I'll try, Reverend Mother. I want to keep faith!"

She smiled and nodded, then, motioning Catherine to stay seated, she got up and moved about briskly, pouring hot milk from a pot heated over a charcoal brazier into two metal tankards. To this she added ale, honey, and several spices. Catherine held hers in both hands, feeling the lovely warmth travel through her body. The Abbess took a long drink of her warm posset, then set it down and leaned toward her visitor, hands clasped in front of her on the desk. "The news you brought me about the destruction of St. Clements was no surprise, Catherine. This will come to pass. I have been so warned." She nodded sadly. "But"—she held up a staying finger —"we may have another year's grace."

"My uncle heard it would be at the turn of the new year."

She shook her head emphatically. "I have it on very good authority that it may be postponed, and in the meantime I will petition the king." The firmness of her words concluded the discussion. "Now, Catherine, I must ask a favor of you. Your coming here may prove a blessing." She thoughtfully moved things around on her desk, as Catherine remembered she did when confronted by a knotty problem. "I want you to persuade Sister Emily that it would be well for her to go to Scotland."

"To Scotland?" Catherine echoed in disbelief.

"Yes. She has a niece in Scotland, prioress of a holy order in Iona. She's offered Sister Emily a home. Quite frankly, it would ease my mind to know that she was well cared for." She sighed and looked at Catherine, her face troubled. "When St. Clements is dissolved she may not be so fortunate."

"I'll take her," Catherine said without hesitation.

"Good. You won't have to go alone. I can arrange for the two of you to travel with the horse caravans that cross Northumberland and up to Scotland, carrying supplies to the castles and abbeys."

"What about the Border reivers?"

The Abbess shrugged. "The Border wars are still going on, but the reivers and mossbacks seldom attack the caravans. The lords and the lairds must have their supplies, and if the traveling chapmen are attacked, they will refuse to journey to those isolated places."

"When would we leave?"

"In two days. That will give you enough time to get some warmer things together."

Catherine nodded her agreement, looking at the Abbess, irrelevantly noticing how the stark, simple cowl and wimple were a proper frame for her thin patrician features and the serenity of her brown eyes. Maybe the Reverend Mother is right, she thought. Scotland! Maybe even now God is showing me the way . . . !

Catherine let herself out into the moon-white world and hurried across the fields. Frost had solidified the muddy pastures, and she stumbled often in the ruts, her eyes fixed on the distant copse of trees. She had fashioned a wreath of the soft end shoots of pine branches, winding them around a circle of wire and fastening them in place with tiny pinecones and clusters of red berries. It gave a bright and happy look to the white wooden marker. She sat on the outcropping of rock, under the big elm tree—bare now of all but its beards of hairy moss—which spread protective arms over the frail undergrowth and the grave of her mother.

The stars were so thick they hung over the land like a silvery canopy, and the night was held in an eerie quiet. A cry broke the silence. She knew it was the cry of a lost sheep caught in the scree on the moor. She had heard it many times before, but the plaintive cry now seemed unearthly, as if it were a lost soul crying for a place of peace and rest. She wryly shook away the grim thought. It was a sheep, she told herself firmly, and if it doesn't stop its bawling, it will make a meal for a hungry wolf before the herdboy can find it in the morning.

She could feel the cold from the rocky seat seeping through the heavy layers of her clothing, but she still sat, one desolate thought tumbling over another. She didn't have to say anything. Her mother knew. She suddenly hugged herself with both arms clasped around her body because there was no one to hold her, then she leaned her head against the rough wet trunk of the old elm tree and wept until she felt completely spent.

CHAPTER SEVEN

The first few days were pleasant enough, but necessarily slow because of the heavily laden horses. Occasionally they would pass the time of day or share their bread and cheese with gray-gowned Franciscans or black-robed Dominicans, walking the muddy roads from cottage to cottage, village to village, to comfort or to perorate, as the occasion demanded. The chapmen traded and bargained at large manor houses and magnificent abbeys: the twelfth-century Fountains Abbey, the magnificent Seventh-century Ripon Cathedral, damaged and repaired through the centuries and housing a hierarchy who lived and ruled like kings amid their rich hunting parks, and the unbelievably beautiful Rievaulx Abbey. The castles they called on—Bowes, Barnard, and Raby—were huge forbidding fortresses, built for defense. The rivers were swift, dark and full of crashing energy. Huddles of sheep looked like gray rocky protuberances against the brown-green hills, wrinkled with gullies and ravines that seemed to climb up into the leaden sky. The land was harsh, poor, and bleak, foreign to the gentle green and rolling land to the south, but it fascinated Catherine with its strangeness.

As they crossed the River Tyne, she experienced a quickening of her pulse. This was Northumberland, a wild country, primitive and barren, a thorn in the king's side because it paid few taxes and stubbornly "answered to no king but a Percy." It was also a place of violent battles and vendettas between marauding Border forces. Moss-troopers raided both sides of the Border and fought among themselves. The English plundered the Scots and the Scots pillaged and burned out the English. The chapmen and archers were now on the alert. The archers adjusted the metal sallets on their heads and retied their leather tunics, which were reinforced with many layers of heavily padded deerskin, allowing them some freedom of movement but somewhat less protection than armor. They all carried swords and leaden mauls in addition to their bows and arrows, and they looked tough and ready for battle.

Darkness fell suddenly as the caravan neared the Border town of Berwick-on-Tweed. Ahead, the narrow ravine looked to be just a darker shadow until horsemen thundered out of its stygian recesses like black harbingers of death and immediately surrounded the caravan, some twelve men strong.

The leader thrust a bill above his head, the axhead glinting sharply in the uncertain light of the moon. "We'll be takin' the goods an' the horses, but we'll no' be takin' y'r lives, if ye mind y'r manners!" he shouted.

"No!" As if on signal the archers and chapmen rushed the raiders, swinging bone-crushing mauls, and slashing and chopping with swords and axes.

Catherine grabbed the reins of Sister Emily's horse and dragged it behind her into the ravine, then placed herself protectively in front of her with her sword drawn. Her heart pounded crazily and her teeth were chattering like castanets as she watched the hideous battle and heard the shouts of the men, the bloodcurdling screams of the dying, the thud of horses' feet and their frantic snorting and whinnying. Sometimes she saw only darker shadows flailing the night, and then the moon would come out from behind a cloud, painting the barbaric scene with picture clarity. The fight was savage and short. The chapmen lacked experience, and at such close quarters the archers had little use of their deadly arrows and were no match for the cunning, seasoned raiders. The little nun hadn't stopped mumbling her distraught appeals to God, and sick and shattered, Catherine motioned her to quiet and drew them farther back into the shadows. The raiders were rounding up the packhorses and shouting their glee at the rich booty.

"Och! Twenty-two horses there ware! Three dead ones lay there! We're a missin' trae!" The leader wheeled around and plunged into the ravine, reining his mount so sharply, it reared up before them, front feet beating the air.

"Don't touch her!" Catherine shouted, bringing her sword up to the ready. "I'm taking this nun to Scotland to escape the king's chopping block!" Her ear had caught the singing lilt of a Scotsman's tongue, and her only hope was to bind them together through mutual hatred of King Henry. The Scotsman looked from Catherine to the nun, who had drawn herself up regally and thrown back the fur-lined hood to better display the headdress of her religious order.

"A Douglas I am, sir. I go to my niece, prioress of a convent in Iona. She's of the powerful Armstrongs!" Her voice captured a suggestion of remembered lilt, and Catherine felt a start of surprise. She had been only "Sister Emily," with no surname, all these years.

"Och! Ane Armstrong! Saints love us!" He beat on his chest. "It's ane Armstrong I am! John the Bald!" He swept off his cap in a courtly gesture, grinning as the moonlight gleamed on his bald pate fringed with hair that fell to his shoulders. He jammed the cap back on and touched the tip of his sword to Catherine's chest, making her shrink back, and a breath of a gasp escaped her. "An' what ware ye thinkin' of, auld woman, choosin' sich a skinny laddie?" He peered at her as he quieted his restive horse. "And a bonnie, high-born ane a' that, who has nae arm for the sword!" With a quick flick of his weapon he sent the one spinning from her hand, then threw back his head and roared with laughter as she got down to retrieve it. Abruptly he was alert and sober. "Come alang! Ye'll ride wi' us, but ye better be faster on t' horse than ye air wi' ye'r sword!"

They rode swiftly through the night, over hill and dale, to the River Tweed, which they crossed on crude rafts that had been hidden in the shallows. There they were joined by another group of horsemen, riding fast, who had been pillaging and burning the outskirts of town, and they rode on together, driving the horses and cattle before them. For the first hour or two there were sounds of pursuit and the chilling baying of bloodhounds, but gradually they became fainter and finally died away. Catherine followed blindly behind Sister Emily, who just as blindly followed the riders in front of her.

Morning was graying the sky, promising a cold, leaden day when they arrived across the Border and into Scotland at the village of the reivers, situated in a protected valley, with a burn in full spate cascading through it. Women and children and men past the age of fighting poured from the great log houses, shouting and laughing as they saw their men safe and the fat contraband to be shared. The center of the big valley held three tall towers—peels—three stories high, to shelter the villagers during times of raid, and the leader indicated with a jerk of his head that the two women were to accompany him to the largest of the three.

Sister Emily's face looked like a death mask as she fell off her mount into the arms of John the Bald, and Catherine was bewildered at his gentle solicitation as he helped her past the massive oak door studded with nails and up the stone stairs to the first floor living quarters. A peat fire smoldered and flickered in a scooped out area in the middle of the stone floor. The room hung with acrid smoke that burned their eyes and made them cough; only a little of it was sucked out through the thin arrow slits in the gray rock walls. But it was warm, and the meat and oatcakes and ale served to them by Enid, John the Bald's wife, satisfied their hunger and they were left to sleep while the booty was divided.

Sister Emily slept the deep sleep of the old and exhausted who trustingly puts her fate into God's hands, but Catherine lay awake far into the night. The sleeping quarters of the peel were above those of the living area. There was no fire, but she was grateful not to have to breathe the acrid peat smoke, and she and the nun were snug in their warm, vermin-free blankets. She could hear faint strains of revelry, which would go on far into the morning, but they had men hidden in the hills, taking turns at guard duty. Filtering into her mind came unbidden thoughts: William has my letter by now, so he knows my shame and my heartbreak. What does he feel? Shock? Disgust? Yes. And perhaps sadness for me. Does he feel any of the terrible emptiness that I do? The loss of something beautiful and irreplaceable, like a piece of my soul that's been cut away? He will marry. A man in his position must. Who would it be? Sheila? A hopeless cry welled up, escaping her lips, and she pressed it into the blanket, fighting to clear her mind to examine the touchy problems at hand. Somehow she had to persuade John the Bald to help them get to Iona. From there she could find her way by boat to the isles of Morven and Mull. He was a hard, restless man with strange, wild currents running through him, and it was difficult to know how to circumvent the ruthless, cruel part of him and appeal to the kinder side she had seen a few times.

John the Bald sat on the floor near the fire, nursing a racking hangover. He carefully raised his head and glowered at them through bloodshot eyes. "A'm no carin' if I kill you." His matter-of-fact statement filled Catherine with corrosive fear. He was having second thoughts about allowing them to go free! The location of their campsite in this wild, remote region was a well-guarded secret. Could he risk trusting two strange women to keep their mouths shut? He was still weighing the idea, but hadn't made a decision. Her thoughts scurried like frightened mice around the walls of her mind. What could she say that would turn the tide in their favor? At this moment it would be useless to appeal to him on the basis of either religion or chivalrous compassion for the weaker sex. Perhaps he would understand her vow for revenge. She would have to take a chance.

"We need a favor from you, John the Bald, leader of the Armstrongs!" Her tone of belligerence stemmed from long and exhausting fear. Fortunately it made her sound bold and self-confident.

There was a tautness about him, as if he was alert to move or to fight at any instant. "Gae on," he murmured.

"I'm a MacRaeggan, the daughter of Lady Anne MacRaeggan, who was violated by the idiot Graham MacOrvan by the order of his father, Sir James MacOrvan." She closed her eyes against the sickness. "I am her daughter by Graham." The heavy silence was like a magnet that drew her eyes open. John the Bald was staring at her with a dawning repugnance. "Sister Emily raised me."

The nun's face was runnelled with lines of pain, as if she knew the agonized effort it cost her beloved Catherine to expose her shame to a stranger, in order to save their lives. "Yes, John the Bald, and she is all the Lord could ask of a young woman." Her voice was choked with tears.

"MacOrvan," he said slowly. "A gey roch lot. Hated by all. Nae here-aboots name. He be a laird o' the isles. Mull. Morven."

"Yes. That's where he is," she whispered, then blurted boldly, "I need your help, John the Bald, to get Sister Emily to Iona. After that I can find my way to Mull."

His laugh had a humorless sound. "Ye're daft, lass! Mebbe anither time. Ye couldna win noo. Tis *geamhradh*—winter. Sae anxious ye air t' set eyes ain ye'r *senair*—grandfather?"

"Yes, I'm anxious to see my grandfather." Her panic had passed, and she felt a rising confidence fed by cold and calculating hatred. "I'm going to kill him!"

He measured her with a long look, and finally he smiled a thin, tight smile, cold and amused, as if revenge were something he understood and approved. "'Tis done!" he said curtly, with a brief nod of his head.

By the order of John the Bald, Catherine and Sister Emily were passed from friendly clan to friendly clan as they were guided across Scotland to the coastal town of Oban. Christmas and Hogmanay came and went, and it was the new year of 1534. Two weeks went by while they waited for the storms to pass and the sea to calm so they could travel down the Firth of Lorne to Iona.

The innkeeper's wife was a friendly soul and fond of weaving brave and chilling tales of Scottish clans, as they sat in front of the peat fire on blustery nights nibbling on fruit fritters and tansy cake. Eventually she told the story of the MacRaeggans and the MacOrvans, and it was easy to encourage the gudewife to talk further about Sir James MacOrvan. He had been married two or three times since then, she said, and was now a widower with a young son, named Richard, after his first son, murdered by the MacRaeggans. "He's a hard an' oogly mon, a mon o' sin!" she said, making the sign of the cross. "He hae nae luv for nae mon, but f'r his bairn, the bonny laddie, Richard, sae sevan years aboot."

"Does this boy have a tutor?" Catherine asked, trying to keep the excitement out of her voice. The woman looked at her blankly. "Does he go to school? Who gives him his schooling?"

"Aweel, now, there ware a monk who gae the bairn his letters f'r a wee time, but he came awa'. I heerd he said it ware a place of evil." She automatically crossed herself again. "An' there ware an auld woman f'r a time, anly the winter fleggit her awa'."

"I'm a teacher. I've taught children Latin, mathematics, and French. Also music. And I'll be looking for a position, to fill in for a few months until I . . . I . . . return to England."

The woman's small gray eyes plainly mirrored her curiosity as to why a beautiful young woman would consider such a place, but she kept her counsel. "Ye canna gae to him. He doesna miss ane thing. He kens wha' and who is aboot. He'll be hearin' of ane teacher in Iona, sae he'll think on it and mebbe he'll be a callin' fer ye."

So that was it, and a wise piece of advice it was, Catherine thought. *If he came to me as a total stranger and made me an unexpected offer, he would have no cause to be suspicious.*

The boat sailed down the Firth of Lorne under clear skies and a spanking wind, past Gylen Castle, which rose protectively at the tip of Kerrera, past the strange Carsaig Arches and around the craggy, precipitous cliffs of the Ross of Mull, where the captain kept his men on the jump as they passed through a treacherous bed of jagged rocks known as the Torrins. Finally they dropped anchor a distance offshore, and Catherine and Sister Emily were transferred to a small boat, along with two monks, and rowed to the little flat island of Iona, which had no true harbor, and were spewed up on the sandy beach like pieces of flotsam.

It was a heartwarming reunion for Sister Emily and her niece, the Prioress, a tall, gentle-featured woman who made her welcome and bade Catherine stay at the nunnery as long as she wished. The days passed quickly for Catherine, at first, as she explored the ancient island, feeling a sense of awe, as if she were walking into the pages of history. She could easily visualize St. Columba, the Celtic monk who had come from Ireland in the sixth century, built a monastery, and preached and civilized as he walked through the Hebrides and Highlands. It was said he was tall and bonny, with a sweet and powerful voice, and through his work Iona became known as the seat of Christianity, the "Canterbury of the Celtic Church," and a place of learning. A great Benedictine abbey and cathedral, with nunneries, now stood on the site of the old monastery. She often walked through Reilig Oran, Scotland's oldest Christian burial ground. There were fifty-three kings buried here, forty-eight of them Scottish, including Macbeth and Duncan, and she tried to visualize them, to put words in their ancient mouths, but she soon tired of this fantasy, and all the doubts, chaotic and unnerving, returned. Maybe her plan wouldn't work and she would have to figure out a new one. Maybe Sir James wasn't interested in a teacher for his son. . . .

Catherine had almost given up hope the day Elton MacOrvan arrived at the nunnery with a note addressed to Mistress Catherine March, from the laird, asking her to accompany his nephew to Mull if she was interested in acting as a teacher or tutor to his son until her contemplated return to England in the spring. He really *did* have his own private source of news, she thought with surprise, and she was thankful she had given the gudewife in Oban her fictitious name of March. She felt a surge of excitement, but aware of Elton's intuitive appraisal, she feigned surprise, a thoughtful consideration, and then asked for more information about the boy, Richard, his father, and the castle. She gave total attention to his terse answers, as if they were completely new to her, and finally agreed to leave with him in the morning.

Sister Emily no longer tried to dissuade her, but she clung to her as if she would never let her go and pressed a rosary fashioned of jet into her hands. "I want you to have it, dear child, and think of me as you say your beads. I'll pray for you every day, pray for your guidance and safety."

"Thank you, dear Sister Emily. I love you. Always know that!" Catherine turned and ran across the sandy beach to the boat where Elton was beckoning to her impatiently and calling out that they would miss the tide if she delayed them any longer.

The early morning was the soft gray of the underwing of a dove and hung with heavy cold mist rising from the smooth, leaden waters of the Sea of the Hebrides. Elton hugged the shore, far enough out to avoid the treacherous rocks but close enough to seek shelter if the brewing storm should break. Except when they were close enough to see the gulls and terns that wheeled and cried around the island cliffs, Catherine felt as if she were floating through a gray amorphous silence. Most of the time Elton kept on the alert as his three companions rowed, but from the impatient lift of his head he was looking for a freshening of the wind to fill out the sails. Once in a while she sensed his scrutiny and looked up to see him staring at her with an air of puzzlement. When her eyes met his, his own widened with an almost imperceptible expression of shock. It must be my *eyes,* she thought worriedly. He must have seen my mother, known her. What will Sir James's reaction be? Thank goodness I dyed my hair!

Daylight was fading as they passed the tip of Ulva and entered Loch na Keal, skimming past the small island in its center. A thrill of torment went through her. *I'm here! I'm here . . . at last!* Her eyes searched the precipitous walls. There it was: Castle MacOrvan! The fortress stood, grim and impregnable, on top of the jagged red-rock cliffs, and she knew there was no welcome for her there. She gripped the seat of the rocking boat and tried to breathe slowly and quietly, but it was impossible with the knocking of her heart echoing loudly in her ears and the trembling within her that made her feel weak and insubstantial.

Elton leaned toward her, raising his voice above the creak of the oars, louder now that they were moving along between the island's walls. "We'll be pulled up then by the ropes, lass. We canna tak' the chance to gae ashore ane the north side of Mull. It would be a takin' too lang, for the storm will be a breakin' aboot now."

Catherine nodded her understanding, hoping her hesitation didn't show as she stared at the sheer, forbidding walls. They shot into a smooth, protected spot and with a thump the keel of the boat slid up on the sand. As she climbed out she heard a faint "Hallooo" from up above, and Elton cupped his hands around his mouth and answered back. Ropes were sent down, and a rough, flat seat, willow-woven, the edges strengthened with hazel. Elton tied her on the seat and handed her a long, stout stick.

"There's naethin' to fear, lass. 'Tis fair smooth, this pairt of the cliff, but ye must be watchin' ye don't get too close. If ye do, use the stick, then, in pushin' yersel' awa'."

She was pulled up very slowly, and she strained to see through the gathering darkness, but all she could make out was the mass of darker wall, so she held the stick out at all times. Occasionally it hit the rock and sent her swinging back out into nothingness, and her heart dropped down into her soggy shoes. As she neared the top, strong hands reached down and drew her up to stand shakily on the ground. Five men stared openmouthed at her in the lanterns held above their heads. She quickly searched the faces. No, her grandfather wasn't among them. Two were young, three were older, and they were all dressed like the scullers. "How do you do? I'm Mistress Catherine March. I'm to be a teacher of the young Richard MacOrvan."

A grizzled elderly man stepped forward and touched his bonnet. "*Failte! 's e do bheatha!* A thousand welcomes! Me name is David Donald, lass. Ye'll be waitin' for Elton, then?"

"Yes, thank you." He nodded pleasantly and went back to help haul up the others. She turned almost reluctantly to look at the castle, looming farther up the rise, surrounded by fortresslike walls. She could barely make out the vast phantasmagoria of roofs and thrusting towers and the battlements, those upper parts of the towers, buildings, and walls with their machicolations, corbeling, and crenellations which were of great military importance in defending the castle. Some distance behind the castle there was a high dark mass: Ben More, the tallest mountain on Mull. Catherine held her breath. She could almost hear the silence over everything. The land seemed held in a state of suspension, like a breath indrawn in suspense, waiting for the storm to hit, to tear at it with primitive violence, to scar and burn it with lightning, to lash it with whips of sleet. And the land would revel in the fight, laugh at the puny elements, and after the storm it would send up new grass, trees, flowers, and even the ugly scrub, in the eternal circle of life.

"Come alang wi' me now, Miss Catherine." Elton's voice cut across her thoughts. "The laird'll be a waitin' for ye."

He'll be waiting for me? Was he so sure I would come? Men walked at her side, lighting her way up the rocky path. She held her skirts up away from the grasping fingers of the scree and bracken and occasionally she felt the sting of the brambles on her arms and legs. They skirted the moat to the front of the castle, which faced into the island. The drawbridge was down and men stood at either side of the high, heavily fortified entrance, holding lanterns. She had just taken her first steps along the gigantic wooden bridge reinforced with mammoth bands of metal when a jagged flash of lightning snaked across the black sky, followed by an earsplitting clap of thunder. The skies split open and violent gusts of wind suddenly flailed them with icy sleet, and sent them running for shelter.

Catherine stood in the gatehouse watching the drawbridge creak back up and close like a giant mouth. She could be the mouse caught in a trap. She shook away the feeling and looked around. This was an ancient castle, with none of the softening elegance of a Whitehall, or the manor houses of Fair Meadows or Birchmont. It had been built for protection of the laird and his family. Horses and fodder and castle supplies were kept here, she noticed as she followed Elton out into the walled courtyard, where he had to take her arm to guide her through the howling blizzard and into the main keep. There they climbed up a narrow spiral stairway built of the same stone as the dour gray walls, and came out into the Great Hall. She shook off her fur-lined cloak and handed it to a small wizened servant, who seemed to materialize out of the shadows.

"I be Thomas," he quavered with a bob of his head. "*Failte! 's e bhur beatha!*"

"Thank you, Thomas." She was shaking so hard, she half staggered over to and collapsed on a stool in front of the massive fireplace, and held her hands out, hoping to thaw out the icy chill that came more from her mind and heart than from her flesh.

"Ach, 'tis been a gey lang trip, then, lass. I'll be fetchin' ye a hot drink."

She looked around at him and smiled her gratitude. He was a thin, twisted stick of a man, his old monkeylike face sallow and intelligent—or was it cunning? He stiffened as though suddenly nailed to the floor, his eyes fairly starting from his head. She schooled her face and voice to a smile. "Is there something wrong, Thomas?" She rubbed experimental fingers over her cheeks. "Do I have dirt on my face from the climb?"

He shook his head like a dog coming out of the water. *"Ha nyall, Ha nyall!"* In a dazed whisper he reverted to the Gaelic "No." "'Tis anly yer eyes . . . sich a green as I've nae seen afore! I'll be a gettin' yer drink." He hurried away with a tottering, lopsided scuttle that reminded her of a multilegged insect.

It's my mother's eyes! He knew, too! She looked around, trying to calm the sick lurch of her heart. The long stone floor was covered with rushes, the few heavy pieces of furniture were old dark wood rubbed with beeswax to a soft patina. There was one chair, an intricately carved Erasmus chair and footstool near the fireplace; the colors in the Flemish wall tapestries were muted and dulled by the peat smoke of many years, as were the heavy red draperies closed over two Gothic windows that must look out onto the courtyard. Above the twelve-foot fireplace was the MacOrvan coat of arms woven into a tapestry, and flanking it were banners, colors faded in streaks, that must have been carried by MacOrvan ancestors in the wars of a century or two past. She got up to study the coat of arms. *The coat of arms of my family,* she thought with a sick shiver. She peered closer. There was a Celtic cross, so the MacOrvans were Celts . . . and a scepter . . . and the animal looked like a unicorn . . . or maybe . . .

"Ah, Miss March! Are you interested in coats of arms . . . heraldry?" The voice, deep and resonant and slurred slightly at the edges, went through her with the pain of a thousand needles. As she forced herself to turn slowly, composedly, she applied a smile.

"Yes, I find them extremely interesting, sir. Sir James, is it?" She hoped he would never guess the effort it cost her to appear self-possessed. Blood drummed in her ears and brought a hot flush of color to her neck and face, but she kept smiling. She felt the tautening of her muscles. The next few minutes would decide the success or failure of her masquerade.

He gaped at her wordlessly, as the tankard of wine fell from his nerveless fingers. He looked as she imagined he would: tall, well built, with springy silver hair, thick black eyebrows, and eyes like two pieces of blue ice. His weather-ruddy face, once uncommonly handsome, was etched with the graph of a dissolute life.

"Who . . . who are you?" he demanded in a whisper.

"I'm Catherine March. You sent for me."

He made an abrupt dismissing gesture with his hand. "Where do you come from? Who are your parents?"

"I'm from London, daughter of Sir George March and his wife, Lady Gwendolyn."

He stood, feet planted apart, eyes narrowed as he studied her hair and her face with an insulting intensity. Then his gaze traveled over her body with slow deliberation. Their stares were locked for a long moment before he nodded toward a stool and sat down in the Erasmus chair. She felt a profound disquiet that was rapidly mounting to naked fear, and she was relieved to sit and steady her trembling. "I know your father, then. We attended the same schools in England. How are they . . . Sir George and Lady Gwendolyn?" His voice was still hoarse, but the words were studiedly casual.

He's trying to trip me up. They've both been dead long enough for him to hear about it since he travels often to England! She gave him what she hoped was a glance of surprise. "My parents have been dead for some six years now, Sir James. Plague."

"Ah! I'm sorry to hear that. Your sister? Her name escapes me . . ."

"You must be thinking of another family, Sir James. I have only an older brother, Philip."

"Ah, of course. I recall him now." He glared suddenly at a point past her shoulder and she turned to see Thomas holding a tray with a cup of steaming liquid. Sir James impatiently gestured him away, but Catherine called him back.

"Thomas! I'll have it here, please." She looked at the rakish, glowering laird. "If you don't mind, Sir James . . . I'm badly chilled."

His black bushy eyebrows met in a frown, as if he resented having an order countermanded by a slip of a girl. "Of course." He nodded curtly to the manservant, who had been hovering uncertainly behind her. He came around immediately and handed her the cup.

"Thank you, Thomas." Her smile brought the color flooding into his monkey face, and he gave her a quick bob of his head before he picked up the tankard the laird had dropped.

"Would ye be wantin' a drink, m'lud?"

"Yes. Wine," he answered without taking his eyes off her. She felt a sting of anger. What a rude bully he was! The little servant was obviously scared half out of his wits. The anger suddenly made her calmer. She sipped the hot posset while Sir James drank his wine, still watching her broodingly.

"Your given name is . . . Catherine?"

"Edna Catherine. I was called Edna while I was growing up, but I prefer Catherine." Fortunately, the life of Sir Howard Walker's nurse, the late Edna March, had been discussed at some length after her tragic death from the plague and Catherine was thankful she knew enough about her to assume her identity for a while. It was too recent a happening—she hoped—for Sir James to have heard reports of it.

"And your brother, Philip? He was rather a reckless young man, so I understand."

"Yes, I'm afraid so. But I think he is now 'turning over a new leaf,' as they say. He has gone to the Indies to invest in a business."

"Invest?"

"A friend is putting up the money. Philip has none." Phew! I was almost trapped that time, she thought in a panic. Their conversation was that of two swordsmen: thrust, parry, and riposte, and so far she had barely been able to hold her own. He continued the interrogation and she managed to answer readily enough. She had enough knowledge of herbs and nursing to get by; she knew Sir Howard Walker, the physician who had employed Miss March as a nurse, so she sounded bona fide.

Supper was served to them in a small dining area adjoining the Great Hall, and the food was brought up to them from the underground kitchen. Hot and tasty vegetables, bannock cakes with fresh butter, and a great poached salmon that was as well prepared as anything she'd eaten at Birchmont Hall were served with a bramble-berry tart that melted in her mouth. At first she had to force herself to eat so she wouldn't appear nervous and ill at ease to this man she so despised and feared, but soon her healthy young appetite, sharpened by the long boat trip, took over with a relish. There was a feel of luxury about the table even though it wasn't covered with a cloth. The beautiful wood was highly polished, white linen napkins, spoons, and forks were set beside the handsome pewter plates, and the wineglasses were of fine Venetian crystal. It was as if the laird wanted to keep the castle and furnishings—things of his heritage—unchanged but indulged his taste for luxury in the smaller, personal things.

"Take off your headdress, Miss Catherine."

She looked up with a start from the last bite of brambleberry tart. "My headdress?" she echoed in surprise.

He nodded, his intense blue eyes compelling her to do his bidding. With a fast-beating heart she removed the bodkins that held it in place, and as she drew it off, her dark auburn hair fell around her. She shook her head so it fell down her back and she smoothed it away from her face. The ragged suck of his breath sent a stab of fright through her. Was he seeing her mother, in spite of the difference in hair color? With growing apprehension she suddenly realized her precarious position. She had cut herself off completely from everyone, and she was alone and at the mercy of this laird in his ancient, isolated castle. The silence grew larger, like a living thing, feeding on his suspicion and her fear. When she could stand it no longer, she said:

"Am I to meet my pupil this evening, Sir James?"

His expression immediately softened. "Yes, when he's finished his supper."

"He takes supper in his room?"

"Except for a special occasion. He keeps to a schedule, Miss Catherine. Breakfast at seven o'clock in either the dining room or kitchen, lessons until the midday meal, which he takes with me . . . us. Afternoons are free for fencing, archery, riding . . . whatever his pleasure or the weather dictates." He put his elbows on the polished table top, rested his chin on his pressed-together fingertips, and regarded her coldly. "You do not approve, Miss Catherine?"

She put her fork down, and it seemed to clatter loudly against the pewter plate. "I do not presume to disapprove, Sir James. But at seven years of age isn't some four and a half or five hours of study a little too long for him?"

He gave an impatient shrug of one shoulder, and the beautiful emerald brooch pinned to his tartan glowed like fire in the candlelight. "If you feel unable to teach and encourage his eager, bright young mind, please say so now! You are well versed in Latin, mathematics, French . . . and you have taught other children, as I was informed?"

"Yes, of course. I have been both a nurse and a teacher. What about music? Religion?"

"Music, if he so wishes. I take care of his religious training."

"Very well." The silence grew heavy again. He was not the sort of man who felt the need to fill silence with a spate of unimportant chatter. The servingman filled his wineglass again, and she shook her head at his offer to refill hers. "I still have some, thank you." She couldn't seem to avoid the laird's steady, brooding eyes, so she turned to examine the wall of books and was delighted to see he had an excellent library. There were several of Chaucer's books: *Canterbury Tales, Troilus and Criseyde,* and *Parlement of Foules;* and Sir John Mandeville's *Travels,* Sir Thomas Malory's *Morte d'Arthur,* which she was anxious to read. There was also a Latin-English dictionary, the first she'd ever seen; a Bible, and The New Testament, in an English translation, which was banned in England because it was considered heresy.

"This time I see you do approve, Miss Catherine!" He inclined his head slightly, studying her with mock intensity.

"Oh yes, sir! You have a very fine collection."

"Even The New Testament . . . *in English?*" He held the palms of his hands together in a saintly mimicry and rolled his eyes toward heaven.

He's baiting me! she thought testily. "I don't know for sure if the Church has declared against it, or not, but I am aware that William

Tyndale translated the words of St. Paul, as: 'faith, hope and love,' while the bishops rule it should have been: 'faith, hope and charity.' To my mind, charity is a form of love . . . one form . . . but of course, love has many forms. Don't you agree, sir?" He said nothing, but she caught a glint of grudging admiration in his intense blue eyes. "I care not in the least if it is banned by King Henry. That only makes me more interested in reading it." She picked up her wineglass and pretended to sip a little, seeking something to shield her face from his unflickering stare.

He started to speak, finally, but broke off at the sound of footsteps, and the softer look was again on his face. A young boy stood in the doorway, flanked by two large deerhounds with dark blue-gray shaggy hair. The dogs bounded in, barking excitedly, going to Sir James to be patted, then they warily circled Catherine's chair, sniffing and growling low in their throats. She sat still, waiting for them to get acquainted before she made any overtures.

"Prince! King! Down!" The boy walked to her chair, and the dogs, still grumbling, obeyed.

"This is Miss Catherine March, Richard. My son, Richard, Miss March." The boy made her a charming, slightly formal bow as they exchanged amenities, but he didn't smile or seem particularly pleased to see her, and he regarded her steadily as he politely answered her questions. He was tall for his years, thin and wiry, with no vestiges of rounded cheeks or baby fat. He looked to have been born at this age in a miniature image of his father, with intense blue eyes, sooty lashes, and a close cap of black silken hair that curled like soft feathers all over his well-shaped head. His eyebrows were delicate now, but would bush later and arch and frown to suit his mood. He stayed only a few minutes, then gave his father a perfunctory kiss on the cheek and said, "Good night, sir," inclined his head to Catherine: "Good night, Miss Catherine," and went out into the Great Hall and up the spiral staircase, followed by his four-footed companions.

"He's a handsome, strong-looking lad."

An expression of pride so fierce as to be painful passed over his face. "Yes. He will make his mark in this world, one day." The love in his voice touched her for a moment and she had to consciously fight against the magnetism of this man. But the moment passed, replaced quickly by the old hatred as he discussed her duties, an outline of study he expected her to follow, and the hours she would have free, all the while drinking copious amounts of wine. The florid undercast of his weathered face—which indicated high living and hovering apoplexy—rapidly deepened, and now his eyes were aware of her as a beautiful young woman. Under her fright and revulsion she felt the sudden drag of intense fatigue.

"May I be excused, Sir James? I'm very tired. It's been a long day."

There was a flash of amusement in his eyes as he superciliously elevated one dark eyebrow. "Don't fret . . . young Miss March." His thickened tongue slurred the words. "I brought you here to teach my son, not to warm my bed!" He bent his head in a mocking bow and his laughter filled the room with its depravity. It stopped abruptly as he bellowed, "Thomas!" The little man popped in immediately from his seat on the kitchen stairs.

She followed Thomas through the Great Hall to the stairway entrance flanked by a display of broadswords, dirks, lochaber axes, the frequently used heavy sword of the highlander—the claymore—with quatrefoil terminals to its quillons. They went up the narrow stone stairway, which rose in a clockwise spiral, so the laird or a defender had his right arm free to pick off attackers one at a time with sword or the heavier claymore. How many bloody battles have been fought on this stairway through the centuries? Catherine thought with a shiver. How much blood had seeped through the rushes, to leave its stain forever embedded in the stone floor? She shook away her macabre thoughts. The long stone hall was bitterly cold, and stronger drafts made the candles waver and grow. They passed several heavy oak doors before he stopped at the last one at the end of the corridor.

The large square room was still cold in spite of the peat fire that burned brightly in the fireplace. But at least it added a cheerful note to the dark hangings and heavy furniture and the sound of sleet being hurled against the window with torrential force.

Catherine lay shivering, the covers up tight around her chin. The linen sheets had been like ice when she crawled in, but the heated bricks she had wrapped and put at her feet felt heavenly. She drew one up with her toes and held it in her arms, and gradually she could feel tense muscles unknot themselves. She looked around the room at the floor-to-ceiling tapestries, which seemed to have absorbed their dark, somber colors from the cold stone walls. The one window had recently replaced iron bars, and fingers of the wild wind forced their way around ill-fitting corners, stirring the heavy drapes into ghostly moving shadows. Above the smoky peat smell was the cloying, unhealthy smell of damp ancient stone. These thick old walls, wherein murder had once been a commonplace fact of life, were security against the storm.

Her thoughts shifted. Sir James MacOrvan is my *enemy*. And I must know my enemy's habits and moods thoroughly. And I must find his weak spots, so he can never take me—but I can take him—by surprise! His son, Richard, is his greatest weakness. But I can't hurt him through a child without hurting the child himself. Drink! That's the most plausible. I can slip some poison into his wine, but I must know his habits and gain his confidence, and that of Richard, and most of all Thomas, who never seems to be far away from the laird. Then I can move around freely. The thoughts that milled around in her mind were dark and macabre, and abruptly, the one she'd been pushing into the back of her consciousness broke free. "My father . . ." she whispered into the echoing darkness. "Is he still . . . alive? How can I find out? Whom can I ask? Where would he be? Will I ever see him?" She shuddered involuntarily, and a premonition of tragedy followed her into a restless sleep.

She awoke to trembling terror, completely disoriented by the dark, not remembering for a moment where she was. She lay stiff, listening, every taut nerve alert to the least noise. It was the quiet she heard. The storm was over, and now there was a different sound: far below she could hear the roar of the waves as they smashed and clawed at the spume-wet cliffs like giant demonic hands. She hated the laird; she hated being here; she hated these cold stone rooms and this castle, and they hated her back. This pile of ancient stones had always protected its lairds, and she was an interloper, a would-be assassin, and they would find a way to destroy her! She wanted to get up and run as far and fast as possible. She wanted to run to William . . . to his dear, strong, and protective arms! An agony, too deep for tears, tore at her until she felt raw with pain. The magic of love had touched her . . . oh, so briefly . . . and she would never be the same again. What was he doing now? Did he miss her as she missed him, with all her heart and soul? She couldn't have him . . . ever . . . but she couldn't stop loving and wanting him any more than she could stop her heart from beating. And Tansy . . . had she married? She would give anything in her power if Tansy could be sharing this room, leaning on one elbow as she looked up at her from the truckle bed and calling a spade a spade in her own inimitable, down-to-earth way. . . .

It was still dark on the first morning when Catherine hastened through the cold, echoing halls, so she had to light her way down to the kitchen with a candle. As she opened the big oak door, she felt as if she had stepped into a different world, a friendlier, more comforting world of light and blessed heat and the chatter and bustle of ordinary people going about ordinary tasks. It was a huge place, dug under the earth, with a cobblestone floor, no windows, and three immense fireplaces, with ovens at the sides for baking. Racks of lamb were turning on the spits, two pots were being stirred, and heavenly fragrances hung in the smoky air. As she hesitated, Thomas popped up and scuttled toward her.

"Och! Come ben the hoose! Come awa' in, Miss Catherine!" He indicated a bench at the table where Richard sat eating his breakfast, the two big deerhounds at his feet.

"Thank you, Thomas!" She smiled at him, and again color flushed his cheeks before he bobbed away. "Good morning, Richard." The dogs rumbled a throaty warning.

He immediately got to his feet with a small bow. "Good morning, Miss Catherine!" He stood, unsmiling, until she was seated before he sat down. "King! Prince! Quiet!" The rumbling stopped. "Did you rest well?" he asked politely, applying himself to his oatmeal, really not caring, she was sure.

"Yes, thank you. After the storm died down."

He nodded but didn't look up. "The wind howls a lot. If you're not used to it, it could be upsetting."

What a strange little boy! She felt as if she were conversing with a man. Thomas put a bowl of steaming oatmeal before her, along with a glass of foaming fresh milk, a pitcher of cream, and a dish of brownish sugar. The oatmeal had a different smoky-peat taste that gave it added flavor, and with sugar and cream it took her back to her early childhood at St. Clements before the nunnery felt the pinch of poverty. As she ate, Thomas brought the cooks and menservants over, one after another, to introduce them to the new teacher, and they gave her a hearty welcome. There was no diffidence in their manner. They were Scots, proud and a little cocky about it, and their eyes openly mirrored their appreciation of her beauty.

It was nine and a half of the clock when the sun came up and flooded the schoolroom with light. Catherine blew out the candles and got up and stretched. "Get up and stretch, Richard." They had been working steadily for the past two hours. She had tested him in every subject she would be teaching him and found him very advanced, with a curious, eager mind that was like a sponge the way it soaked up and retained knowledge. It was going to be a pleasure to instruct him.

"Very well." He got up and stretched and walked around the room. The hounds padded behind him. As they neared Catherine, the low growling started.

"Now, look here, Prince . . . King," she said in laughing exasperation, "I'm going to be with your young master every day and you may as well get used to me!" She made fists of her hands and held one out to each dog, knuckles up. The hounds hesitated, still grumbling as they sniffed, but finally the larger, King, licked her hand tentatively and Prince followed suit. Then they allowed her to pet them, and she did so, carefully, and stopped before they got nervous. There was a ghost of a smile on Richard's lips, but he said nothing.

They ate their midday meal alone in the dining room, served by a garrulous manservant. It seemed that the nephew, Elton, had gone with the laird to Oban, where the laird had business. And they would bring back the horse, Dileas, which she had left to board with the gudewife. To Oban, on such a day? Travel on the icy crude roads would be precarious at best! And he knew the name of my horse! She had a distinct feeling of uneasiness. Was there nothing that escaped Sir James? Obviously he had his own methods of finding out everything, so how could she hope to fool him with this false identity? She tried to recall if the gudewife had seen her hair its original black. She had arrived in Oban dressed as a young man, with her hair covered with a flat cap. Could the gudewife have seen any strands sticking out? Was she that observant? Sister Emily had helped her to dye her hair, and they did it behind the closed bedroom door. Had they left any traces of dye in the basin? They had washed it out so carefully!

Oh, stop borrowing trouble, she chastised herself sharply. You'll have to face it and handle it if the time comes! She was suddenly aware of Richard's scrutiny. Had he read the worry on her face? "Well, Richard," she said brightly, "what are you going to do this afternoon?"

He shrugged. "If Elton were here, I would take a fencing lesson." He looked out the window. "If the ice melted, I would go hunting hares, but"—he shrugged again—"I will probably read."

"Would you do me a favor?"

"Certainly, if I can."

"Would you show me around the castle?" She held her breath and waited. If she knew the layout of the castle, she might be able to find out where her father was, if he was still alive.

He regarded her silently for a moment, then finally nodded. "Certainly. I'd be pleased to." As she followed him out of the dining room, watching the proud set of his handsome head of black silken curls, she thought again what a strange child he was. Perhaps his childhood had been sapped by the lonely solitude of the castle fortress and the lack of companions of his own age. He had the mature qualities of self-possession, of stillness, the arrogance of not needing the friendship or caring of another human being, except, perhaps, that of his father. She thought of the teasing and boisterous warmth of the young Tom and Jack Birchmont. She would feel more comfortable if this boy were more like that. But perhaps it was better that he was reserved, aloof, because she had no intention of becoming fond of him! She had no place in her life, or heart, for this young MacOrvan. . . . She silenced a bitter laugh.

It was well named a castle fortress because, to Catherine, it appeared impregnable. There was a protective system of walls—walls within walls—further guarded by their towers. The gatehouse she came through, the first night, after crossing the drawbridge, was the entrance of the outer circle of walls—or bailey. The main keep was part of the inner circle of walls, and towers rounded the corners of both. Boiling pitch could be poured down from the battlements of the gateways, the towers, and the main keep; and the number of arrow slits attested to the furious onslaught that would greet any foolhardy invader.

Catherine wore her fur-lined cloak because fires burned only in the living quarters of the main keep. Richard told her that once the castle had housed several hundred people but now there was no more than one hundred and fifty to care for the laird and his island stronghold. That, of course, did not include the crofters and their families and the herds who cared for the sheep. She slipped around icy courtyards, walked through cold and empty rooms; climbed spiral stairways, hanging on a rope when the stairs narrowed and steepened, and peered down from battlements.

"This is called the 'Laird's Lug,' Miss Catherine." He walked to an opening near the door to the Great Hall. "It's a listening hole. The lairds of old could listen to the criticism of guests or the servants' grumblings without being seen. My father doesn't use it, of course, but it's an amusing antiquity."

She examined the opening, cleverly concealed between tapestries, and made the proper noises of interest, thinking once more how distressingly mature he sounded. He had the poise and vocabulary of a well-educated man instead of a slip of a boy who would turn eight in the spring. She wanted to take hold of those thin, broadening shoulders and shake some boyish curses or laughter out of him.

They went through the courtyard to the chapel, situated on the outside wall. It was a smaller, perfect replica of an early Gothic cathedral, with a high stone arch, flying buttresses, stained glass windows held in expanses of stone tracery, and a ceiling that culminated in exquisite fan vaulting. She walked slowly down the aisle, genuflected, and crossed herself, then found a place in the rows of benches and kneeled to pray. She didn't ask forgiveness for what she was about to do; she asked only for a ray of hope for herself and a long life of peace and happiness for William and all the others she loved. It was cold, but the stillness, the gloomy serenity, even the musty odor of age-old humanity mixed with dust, damp stone, and incense, had an oddly soothing effect. She seemed to become one with all those people through the centuries who had brought their troubles, hopes, and dreams to this hallowed spot.

She felt a lift of her spirits as they left the chapel, but when they stood at the entrance of the dungeon—dug out underneath the back of the main keep—she felt it drain away. They descended the steep stone stairs, and it seemed as if they were going deep into the bowels of the earth. The feeble light of the guttering candle circled only her feet with its uncertain light; ahead was darkness, behind was darkness. Her heart was beating fast and she could hear her uneven breathing in the utter stillness. Finally there were streaks of light ahead and they came to rest on level rock.

Sun streamed through the high, narrow windows, stamping a pattern of iron bars on the floor, but did little to dispel the gloom of the huge stone room, dripping with wetness. It was bitter cold, and the small wind through the bars whispered in her ears of diabolical deeds as she looked at the chains driven in the walls, at the ghastly tools of torture, rusty with time and the dampness. But it was the huge block of wood, cut from some ancient tree, that made her cry out in horror. The surface and sides were stained with great black blotches that once had been red. Leaning against it was a broad-headed ax, waiting in malignant silence for the executioner's hand.

She turned and ran, tripping over her skirts as she stumbled blindly up the stairs and raced to the warm sanctuary of the schoolroom, a short way down the hall. She was leaning against the wall and drawing gulps of air into her lungs when Richard came in, followed by the two hounds.

He regarded her soberly. "You were frightened, Miss Catherine."

"Yes, I was frightened!" she cried shakily. "That's a dark . . . evil . . . place, where the past will never die! How can men do such horrible things to one another? How?" Her voice ended in a dry sob.

He frowned. "I shouldn't have taken you there. But you wanted to see everything!" His tone carried a note of censure.

"Oh, it's all right, Richard. Really!" she hastened to assure him. "I do want to see everything! It's only that I've seen so many dead in England. And that chopping block—" She broke off. It wasn't only those she'd seen, it was the thought of the dead of all her Clan MacRaeggan impaled around Castle Gullhaven, on the order of this boy's father and her grandfather that filled her with sick horror!

"Richard, there's still something I didn't see."

He came to a halt but didn't turn around. "What's that?"

"The towers. The towers of the main keep," she said.

He turned so she saw his profile. "Oh, no one goes up there, Miss Catherine." He squatted down on his haunches and examined minutely an ear of his hound, King, which appeared to be torn. "The stairs are too dangerous. The stones are cracked and crumbling, so my father has forbidden their use."

"Oh, I see. Well," she said with false heartiness, "I guess they're much the same as the others. And I do thank you, Richard, for showing me the castle. I've never been in a castle before, and I found it fascinating."

"You're welcome, Miss Catherine," he said as he straightened up, and he gave her a long, level glance before he left the room.

She felt a surge of excitement. Many of the stairs she had climbed today were worn in the centers, but the stone was too hard to crumble. *If my father is living, he must be in one of those towers!*

She had supper in her room, wrapped in her warm red woolen

robe. Later she extinguished the candles and by the fire's light found her way to a bench by the window and pulled aside the heavy drapes. She could distinguish only darker outlines of the rounded towers at either end of this back part of the keep, but if someone climbed the tower stairs, she would be able to see a flash of light as he passed the arrow slits in the walls.

Sir James would be away possibly for a week. She would somehow have to try to locate her father before then. She felt a sick reluctance at the spine-chilling thought, but if he was alive, she had to see him! She could never bring herself to believe or accept the fact that Graham MacOrvan was an idiot until she saw him with her own eyes! And, somehow, she also had to see Castle Gullhaven. It was just on the next small island—she could see the island from here—but it might just as well be a hundred miles away. In this kind of weather no one left his home unless it was necessary. It was frustrating to realize it would take longer than she had thought to carry out her plan!

Warm and replete with food, she could feel her eyelids drooping, and she was thinking of going to bed when she was jerked into wakefulness by a faint sliver of light. As she stared wide-eyed, it disappeared, to reappear seconds later, higher up. She saw it twice again, and then there was only darkness. The top of the tower was solid stone. If it had a window it would be facing the loch, and visible only from the loch or the opposite island. She sat on the edge of the bench, watching for what seemed a long time, and then her patience was rewarded. There was a thin flash of light, this time moving down the tower wall. Why would someone go to the top of the tower at this time of the evening if it wasn't to see someone? Perhaps to take a prisoner his food! They certainly wouldn't store anything in the towers! On further examination, as she crawled, cold and shivering, into bed, the entire fabric of her overly active imagination seemed completely implausible. She hugged the covers tight around her. "I won't rest until I find out if he's still there!"

Catherine spent the next two days in an agony of suspense, trying to figure out a way to get up to the tower. First, she had to get the key, and she had no idea which one it was. Keys were not used on most of the immense doors, but those more recently hung, like that at the bottom of the tower, had keys. There were a lot of keys on a board, hanging on the wall near the kitchen stairs, but which one belonged to the tower? By the third evening she knew she couldn't wait any longer, she had to take a chance.

She had supper in the dining room, with Richard, whom she had asked to join her the past two nights. She talked in nervous spates, as if a dam had been opened, and the words flowed out like water, without pause. At first his eyes were wide and inquiring in his listening face, but their expression changed to fit every aspect of the tales she spun. And then, as if caught up in a surge of contagious pleasure, he started to talk. With one word tumbling over another, he talked about his Powy's cob horse, named *Mo Charaid,* Gaelic for "My Friend," and his peregrine falcon, whose Gaelic name was *Geal Or,* meaning "White Gold," and how he raised his deerhounds, Prince and King, from newborn pups, after their mother was killed by a poacher's arrow. For the first time, perhaps because he was away from the disciplined vigilance of his overpowering father, he seemed like a boy of almost eight.

When Richard got up, somewhat reluctantly, to go up to his bedroom, she told him she would be working late again in the schoolroom, preparing ahead for his lessons. The schoolroom was on the same level as the dining room and Great Hall, but at the back of the main keep and near the entrance to the tower.

"Good night, Miss Catherine." He tried for the usual flat politeness, but laughter tugged at the corners of his mouth and broke out into a grin.

She smiled back at him. "Good night, Richard. Sleep well." For one disconcerting moment she wanted to hug him, but shook the impulse irritably away.

In the schoolroom, she tried to read the time away but was too tense to concentrate, so, after reading one page over and over again, she gave up and just sat, stiff with apprehension, listening for footsteps. It wasn't long before she heard Thomas' unmistakable quick, shuffling step . . . but . . . wait . . . there were others with him! Well, it couldn't be helped, she would have to go ahead, as planned.

She hurried to the window and watched the ascending flashes of light, which were stronger this time. They must be carrying lanterns, and there had to be three people.

She cautiously opened the door, closed it softly behind her, then raced in her stocking feet through the corridors and around to the Great Hall, then through the dining room, to the board holding the keys. Her eyes quickly spotted the missing one right at the end. She made a mark on the paper she carried and raced back to the schoolroom, slid in the door and closed it, sagging against the warm wood until she caught her breath. Again she listened at the door, and it had to be more than half an hour before she heard footsteps—heavier footsteps. The fire had died down, so she opened the door a little and put her eye to the larger crack, straining to see, but, to her bitter disappointment, they must have turned the corner, heading toward the Great Hall.

But what was that sound? She recklessly poked her head out, listening. It was the odd sound of metal dragging on stone. The sound suddenly went through her like an excruciating shock. Chains! That's the only thing it could be! "Oh, my God!" she moaned. "It must be my father!" Her mind tried to soften the shock. It could be another prisoner . . . Holding prisoners was commonplace! But she knew, as the cold hackles of dread rose over her skin, that Graham MacOrvan was alive and kept a prisoner in the tower! Her head swam with an onrush of faintness and she sank to her knees, shuddering with abhorrence.

Thomas' smile of welcome faded as he greeted her at the kitchen door the next morning. "Och! Wha's this now! Sae ye didna' sleep well, then, lassie?"

She gave him a wry smile. "I'm afraid not, Thomas. The wind, you know. As Richard says, 'If you're not used to it, it can be upsetting.' It gave me a bit of a headache, but I'm sure I'll feel better after breakfast."

"If you want to rest today, Miss Catherine," Richard said, watching her intently as she sat across from him, "I promise to study hard without you."

"That's kind of you, Richard." She patted his hand, and then regretted the impulse when she saw the tips of his ears turn as red as that in the MacOrvan tartan he was wearing. "I'll work it off in no time."

The lessons dragged; the midday meal seemed to drag on and on, but, conversely, she was shocked to realize the time had arrived and that Richard and the dogs were off with Thomas, to the crofters, up toward the base of the mountain. Once a week Richard went with a manservant to oversee a different phase of managing the island stronghold, and, fortunately, this was his day and Thomas was his escort. She felt a tingling mixture of thrill and fear as she watched them out of her bedroom window until she saw them ride across the drawbridge and head up the rise. She sat for a few moments, marshaling her plans, then her hand reached automatically for Sister Emily's rosary, and she said her beads.

The key in her hand felt heavy and cold. The hallway was a narrow, dark tunnel filled with whispering sounds, and she walked on tiptoes, instinctively the intruder. The key stuck in the keyhole, and she couldn't turn it and couldn't get it out. Blind panic exploded through her. She stood back and closed her eyes, and clenched and unclenched her fists. Stop it, you silly jackanapes! Take it slower! She took a deep breath to relieve the heaviness in her chest and tried again, wiggling the key carefully in place, and the door yawned open into a small round room at the base of the tower stairs. It was empty except for some ugly-looking spears and halberds and a suit of armor.

She heard a spine-tingling sound, like a distant drawn-out sigh, and tried to persuade herself it was the wind seeping through the arrow slits. She started up the spiral stairs. Her legs were trembling so, she had to lean against the wall for support; then she continued on up, step by step, the crushing silence broken only by the agonized rasp of her breathing, the uneven pound of her heart. . . .

CHAPTER EIGHT

A fetid stench assaulted her nose, and it became progressively worse as she climbed, but she was so intent on getting to the tower room that she paid it little heed. She could see the top of the stairs, and as her head came higher, she saw a small expanse of stone floor and two stools set on either side of the great oak door. The door was banded with metal and had open oblong bars on the top and a hinged flap at the bottom where food could be passed through. Her entire body was shaking as if the ague were upon her as she walked fearfully toward the door and peered through the bars. She heard a heavy scurrying sound, and she saw he had his back to her and was looking out the window that faced the loch. He had heard someone coming and he chose to turn away.

The thin afternoon sun outlined a tall, magnificent body, and her heart expanded with sudden hope, but then he turned, alert as some wild thing to the surveillance of strange eyes. With a guttural roar he lunged at her, fists upraised in murderous intent, then brought them down crashing against the door, making it vibrate in metallic shudders. She screamed and fell back, losing her balance and sprawling down on one of the stools. She shrank back instinctively against the wall as they stared at each other. The light from the arrow slits above her caught him full in the face and cruelly stripped away the shadowy impression of noble strength and manliness. His head was large and well formed, and bore a shock of the unmistakable curly black hair, but his didn't fit the poetic songs describing this renowned MacOrvan feature—"black and shining as the silken wings of the raven." His hair hung matted and filthy to his shoulders, and his eyes were the deep MacOrvan blue, but had a vacant expression. He wore a dirty MacOrvan tartan wrapped around an equally dirty tunic.

She just stared in disbelief at the huge man who was now shifting from one foot to the other as he uttered an eerie humming
sound. His humming grew louder and louder until it pressed against
her ears, and he started to dance up and down, faster and faster in a
frenzy, his humming breaking into gleeful gurgles. The sound was
so indescribably horrible that terror went through her in convulsive
spasms, leaving her mouth dry and her teeth chattering. Abruptly
she doubled over, as if hit by an intense pain. Her last shred of
hope was gone!

Very slowly she became aware that there was only the sound of
her cries, and, unwillingly, she raised her head. Graham MacOrvan
was grasping the bars and peering at her with his vacant lackluster
eyes, his forehead furrowed in bewilderment. Then he looked beyond her and made guttural, whispered sounds, and she turned to
see Richard, looking small and pinched, huddled on the stairs, his
face ghostly white and drawn.

"I . . . I thought he was . . . dead! They told me he was dead!"

"What are you doing here?" she gasped, horrified. "I thought you
and Thomas were—"

"Thomas' horse got hurt . . . stumbled in a hole. He's in the stable fixing his leg," he murmured tonelessly, without taking his eyes
off the shocking apparition behind the bars. "I saw him once . . .
one night when they took him out for exercise . . . but they told me
he died."

That's where they were taking him the other night—for exercise.
Does Richard know this is his half brother? She felt queer as she
looked from the bright, strong young man to the mindless giant.
How inequitable life was! She shook her head in perplexity and
slowly got up from her seat. "Come, Richard, we had better go back
down." She reached into her pocket and her hand found the piece of
rich plum cake Thomas had wrapped for her, to nibble on later,
when she hadn't the appetite to eat it at the midday meal. She so
desperately wanted to do something for him, and all she could do
for the moment was give him the piece of cake. She unwrapped it
and held it out to him. He looked at her, then at the cake, and
finally reached out warily and snatched it from her fingers. He

stuffed it into his mouth, grunting happily as he tasted its sweetness. A smile broke over his face, showing strong, even teeth. Richard came to her side and stood as if mesmerized, looking at the prisoner. "Come on, Richard," she said, feeling her own flesh crawl. As she turned away, she was held in place by a yank on her hair. Graham MacOrvan held a long curl between his fingers. Her first impulse was to scream, but she was silenced by the dumb wonder in his face as he stroked its silkiness with clumsy fingers. She managed a stiff smile and softly tugged on the tendril of hair to show him she wanted him to let go, and finally, with obvious reluctance, he let it drop.

A shadow seemed to pass over her and Richard, leaving them silent and withdrawn as they hurried down the spiral stairs and out the tower door. She fumbled with the key, and in nervous haste it again defied her efforts.

"Here, I'll do it." Richard took it from her, but his trembling fingers did no better.

"Wheest! An' where hae ye two been, then?" They both jumped at the sound of Thomas' cold, accusing voice and the key clattered to the corridor floor.

Richard's mouth clamped into a straight line as he glared back at the little man. "You told me my brother died. My father told me he died! Why did you lie?" His biting accusation startled Thomas momentarily out of his anger.

"Weel, I—" He broke off and shook his head sadly. "We thought better ye shouldna be knowin' laddie. Tis a brònach sealladh! A sad thing! Nae fit for y'er yang eyes!" He pulled remnants of his anger together and squinted at them suspiciously, finally fastening his gaze on Catherine. "'Tis you, yang lady, who took the key, then?"

"No, I took it!" Richard picked it up and jammed it in the door and locked it with no trouble.

Catherine shook her head. "You were right, Thomas. I took it. I . . . I saw you . . . and the others . . . take him out, the other night. I . . . I was curious," she finished lamely, unsure if he believed her.

His wizened monkey face was inscrutable. "Ary hoose hae its secrets, Miss Catherine. Dinna wander aboot! 'Tis nae for the likes o' ye to be a pryin' and a meddlin'! The laird, he'll be—"

"You won't tell the laird, Thomas! There's no reason for him to know!" Richard commanded with the scowl of his father.

His face went through rapid kaleidoscopic reactions: fear, hesitation, anxiety, obsequiousness, and finally, agreement. "Ah, weel, laddie, mebbe ye're richt!" he sighed. " 'Twould just steer the pot, then. But ye mustna gae there again!" They both looked at him without replying.

"Thomas," Catherine said softly, "the poor creature is filthy. Worse than any animal. It disturbs us both."

He shrugged. "I daurna gae in. He hae the strength of ten!"

"How do you get him out for exercise?"

He shook three fingers in her face. "Thrae men, then, lass! Ane puts the chain on his collar, through the bars—he allows it then, fare he wants t' gae out 'n' aboot. Twa keep their sairds handy. He kens the prick of the saird!"

"When he's out for exercise, I'll help clean the room."

"Och! Are ye *daft,* lass?"

"Have it cleaned, Thomas! I'm sure my father doesn't know how it stinks! It smells worse than McMurrin's pig pen in the winter!"

How could he know if he never goes there? Catherine thought resentfully. He doesn't even want to acknowledge he exists!

Thomas opened his mouth to say something, thought better of it, and gave a brief nod. " 'Tis aboot time tae burn the mattress, tenny rate."

"And the rushes on the floor, and wash the blankets. You must have plenty of extra bedding. And what about his clothes?" Catherine urged.

He gave a sigh of exasperation, his face puckered like that of a worried ancient monkey. "That hae me fair stoomped!" He thought a long moment, then nodded. "Twice afore we slippit him sae juice o' the poppy. Mebbe we can dae it agan." He took the key from Richard and scuttled away with his odd, lopsided gait, shaking his head and muttering under his breath.

Catherine paced her room in her warm woolen robe, stopping occasionally to put a few peats on the fire. It was late, but her chaotic emotions made sleep impossible. Just the thought of slipping into that helpless land of sleep—unhearing, unseeing—made her flesh crawl with goose bumps. She felt safer awake, for the time being. She had sat by the window and watched thin flashes of lights going up and down the tower, so Thomas must be carrying out his young master's orders.

Finally she realized there had been no lights for some time, so Thomas and his helpers must have finished their disagreeable task. Now perhaps she could get the book *Morte d'Arthur* from the dining room without the risk of running into anyone. The two deerhounds knew her footsteps now, so they wouldn't raise a clamor, she hoped, when she passed Richard's door. Maybe reading something interesting would numb this ghastly sense of utter aloneness she had.

The long, dark corridor was heavy with silence and inexplicable menace, and she hurried along, protecting the wavering flame of the candle, her back stiff with resolve not to glance around at the shadowy somethings that seemed to keep pace. The intermittent soughing of the wind was again like the cries of her Clan MacRaeggan, now more plaintive than demanding. Give me time! Time! she whispered silently. She found the book and hurriedly retraced her way back. As she passed Richard's door, her ears imagined another sound. The cry of the wind? No. She stopped, rigid with listening, and she heard it again, faintly, followed immediately by the heavier wind which sent an icy draft along the floor that struck her feet and pierced her ankles. She put her ear to the crack of the ill-fitting door and heard the same crying sound.

She knocked softly and the door shivered under the onslaught of the two big hounds. "Richard! Richard!" she called, but her voice was lost in their barking. She tried the door; it opened, and the dogs were leaping at her in welcome. "Down! Down!" she scolded until they obeyed.

The large room was oppressively unchildlike in its painful neatness, the luxury of graceful French furniture and the beautiful tapestries on the walls and floor, depicting glorious battle scenes at

Agincourt, the War of the Roses, Robert the Bruce leading his clansmen, and Joan of Arc riding to battle. Sir James had spared no expense in making his son feel a king. The fire had burned low, and she felt the chill cutting through her robe. No sound came from the mound of covers as she walked to the bed. "Richard? It's Catherine. Are you awake?"

The mound moved slightly. "Go away!" His thick muffled voice came from under the covers. "You . . . woke . . . me up!"

She pulled the covers down far enough to uncover a red and swollen face streaked with tears. "How dare you . . . hic . . . come in here . . . hic . . . without being invited!" he shouted. "Get out!" He glared at her, his chest still heaving with controlled sobs.

She averted her face. "I couldn't sleep. I needed someone to talk to . . . a friend. And you're the only one I know, here." She stole a glance at him through lowered lashes. He was up leaning on one elbow, staring at her, his chest quieting.

"Well . . . of course, if I can . . . help." He scowled to cover his relief.

"Do you mind if I build up the fire?"

He grabbed his dark blue robe edged with fur and scrambled out of bed. "I'll do it." He made a pyramid of the peats and pumped the bellows vigorously until the flames were licking the dried squares, then they sat down on stacks of sheepskins and held their hands out to the heat. But before she had a chance to say anything, the dogs barked and Thomas walked in carrying a tray with a steaming posset pot and some bannock cakes and honey. There were *two* metal cups! *How did he know I was here?* He's everywhere at once! He must have eyes in the back of his head! Catherine thought as the little man gave her a slight smile and a bob of his head as he put the tray on the floor between them.

" 'Tis a cald nicht for a talkin' without somethin' to be warmin' y'r insides." He scuttled off. "An' a gude nicht to ye both!"

Richard watched him go. "He has the sight, you know, Miss Catherine," he said, as if in answer to her silent question. And, with an inner apprehension, she found herself believing it. He licked the honey off his fingers and threw the rest of the bannock cakes to the drooling hounds, then settled back and looked at her expectantly.

"I—I've never been in a castle before, as I told you," she began hesitantly, "and now that I'm warm and with a . . . friend, it doesn't seem so frightening—" She chose her words with care, hoping to put him in the role of the protector, so he wouldn't think of his own fears.

"Sometimes the winds sound like voices of . . . ghosts . . . calling out to you," he broke in, nodding his understanding.

"That's right! That's exactly how they sound to me! And then," she continued, "to see Graham MacOrvan . . ." Her heart gave a nervous jolt. Had his name been mentioned, so that she would know it? She looked at him sharply, but his face reflected only his own misery.

"He's my . . . half brother. I saw him once before, but only in the dark. Thomas told me he had committed a terrible deed and was kept in the tower for his own protection and so he wouldn't commit more. I didn't know he was . . . daft!" He gave an involuntary shudder, his deep blue eyes drenched with anguish. She looked at him, then away. His was not a healthy childlike dread as created by the telling of ghost stories. He was going through the same fears as she was, but he was too young to handle it.

"I've seen others like him," she lied in a casual voice. "It is said they are punished by God for their sins, but, fortunately, God's wrath isn't visited on their families." She was conscious of the arrested turn of his head. The only sound in the room was that of King, whimpering and jerking his feet as he dreamed.

"It isn't?" His tone was heavy with hope.

"No." She poured them some more of the hot sweetened milk and sipped on hers thoughtfully. "A friend of mine has a . . . a . . . father like that."

"And she's all right?" he asked anxiously.

"Just fine!" She put her cup down, feeling suddenly sick, and concentrated on gathering her robe tighter around her cold legs, so he wouldn't see her own wretchedness. She got up and shook away her need to cry. "Now I've stayed long enough, Richard. It's way past both our bedtimes!"

He jumped to his feet and followed her to the door. The dogs rolled to their feet and padded after him. "Anytime you're afraid, or want to talk to a friend, please come to my room, Miss Catherine."

"Thank you, Richard. You've helped me immensely."

"And, remember, it's only the wind you hear, not ghosts." He grinned at her broadly, then, suddenly, his face sobered and he reached up and gave her a hard hug, then raced back and jumped on his bed. "Good night, Miss Catherine. See you in the morning."

As she walked blindly down the corridor to her room, she could still feel his wiry young arms around her, and she knew, with dread in her heart, that she was coming to love this boy who was part of her own blood. This posed a terrible problem because now she knew she couldn't hurt him, or desert him. . . .

The next few days seemed to fly. There was a new, easier camaraderie between Catherine and her young pupil. They worked hard at the lessons, but they laughed a lot and challenged each other at games and footracing in the courtyard, in front of the startled servants. The difficult times were the afternoons, when they would sneak up to the tower room with sweets and fruits for Graham MacOrvan. He was clean now. He always hummed and danced when he saw them coming and held his hands out through the bars for the treats they brought him, his great face breaking into a happy grin as he stuffed the offerings into his mouth.

"Do you think we could teach him anything?" Catherine asked one day. "Maybe he could be taught to wash his face and hands. That might be a beginning. But . . . how?"

"We could bring up two basins and a pail of warm water and soap," he suggested excitedly. "I could wash out here, as he watches me. Then we could shove a basin of water through his food door and maybe he would mimic me."

They tried it the next day, and after much coaxing on Catherine's part, the giant hesitantly followed Richard's actions. He laughed when he felt the warm water on his face, and then he licked his fingers and frowned because it had no taste. But he finally splashed his face as Richard did, but with such fervor he emptied the basin full of water all over his chest. The wind through the bars chilled his wetness, and he scowled ferociously as he threw the basin across the room. Then, with two tremendous leaps, he cleared the space and jumped up and down on the basin, instantly flattening it to a metal disk, roaring with anger all the while. Depression settled around Catherine like a shroud. She couldn't shake it off, and it followed her into a miserable, fear-racked night.

With a prickling sensation at the back of her neck, she sensed his presence before she turned and saw Sir James standing in the open door of the schoolroom. His upraised hand and the shake of his head indicated he didn't wish to talk, so she went ahead with the lessons as he sat down and watched them until the school period was at an end. Her nervousness soon left her, and she felt a surge of overweening pride in her pupil as he completed every phase of his difficult studies with dispatch and self-confidence.

"Well done, Richard, and my compliments to you, Miss Catherine," he said as he got up to leave and put one hand briefly on his son's shoulder. Oh, why doesn't he hug him, she thought impatiently. He's only a small boy!

"Thank you, sir," Richard replied, his eyes shining. "It's nice to have you home." The laird acknowledged the pleasantry with a brief nod and went out with a swirl of his pleated kilt.

Catherine could scarcely contain herself as the midday meal dragged on because she so wanted to go to the gatehouse stable to see her Dileas, but she hid her eagerness and kept up her end of the conversation. She kept looking at Richard. His eyes sparkled and he laughed often, and even teased her lightly, telling his father how he always bested her at foot racing and every other game. His entire demeanor was so like a young boy's that she was delighted. The laird was pleasant enough, but there was a stiffness behind his affability, a watchfulness in his bright blue eyes, whenever he glanced her way, as if he had something on his mind, a burr under his skin, and she experienced a slow, burning uneasiness. She forgot about it in the joy of seeing her beloved horse again. Dileas nickered and tossed her head when she saw Catherine running toward her.

"Oh, Dileas! I've missed you so!" she cried happily, flinging her arms around her neck and pressing her cheek against the velvety brown nose. "Isn't she beautiful, Richard? And she can run like the wind!"

He looked at her satiny coat, her strong broad chest, and ran expert hands down her long, sturdy legs. "Yes, she's a fine horse, Miss Catherine. She would make a good mate for my horse, Mo Charaid." As they walked back to the keep, he raised his face to sniff the warmer wind. "It's almost spring. We'll soon be able to ride; then I'll have you a race. I'll bet Mo Charaid can beat Dileas!"

"What will you wager?" she challenged with a laugh, stopping short, hands on hips.

"Hmmmm. Let me see. Oh, I know. Any book from my collection."

"Oh, wonderful! I can think of several I would like!" She clapped her hands; then her smile faded. "I . . . what can I wager?"

"Your Bible," he said quickly, his tone giving it far more value than it deserved.

"Done!" She held out her hand, and they shook on it solemnly. It *does* feel like spring, she thought as they walked on. *I can smell it and see it: winter's snow falling from the trees in soft, wet thuds, water rushing down the courtyard gutters, a snatch of birdsong and the softened wind. Spring . . . Where will I be when it comes? Will the laird still be alive?*

The skirts of her brown homespun were soaked from walking in the courtyard, so Catherine changed into the gown of rich green she had made at St. Clements and joined the laird for supper. His eyes narrowed and a muscle tautened along his jawline as he watched her walk to the table and sit down opposite him. He raised his glass, and now his eyes paid tribute to her beauty.

"*Air do shlainte!*" The words were slurred with drink.

"*Slainte!*" she answered, and raised the wineglass to her lips but only pretended to drink. *How could she drink to his good health?* The thought was macabre!

He drank heavily throughout the meal, and her apprehension increased with his belligerency. Something was still sticking in his craw. Had he somehow discovered new suspicions of her identity, or something about St. Clements? Whatever it was, she sensed it wouldn't stay dammed up too much longer, and suddenly it burst out.

"I don't like what's happening to my son!" he snarled thickly.

His mention of Richard was so unexpected, she could only stare at him. "I thought you were pleased with his progress," she said at last.

He made a rasping noise and gave an angry, dismissing gesture of his hands. "His studies are fine! That's the only reason I'm not turning you out this very night! He's getting soft since you came, and I won't have him soft!" he bellowed, pounding the table so hard, the metal jumped and clattered.

"What do you mean, *soft?*" she snapped back. She had an idea what he meant, but she wanted him to define it in exact words.

"Teasing and playing games with the ladies like any stupid jackanapes who hasn't a brain in his head!" he sneered. "My son is going to learn to live in a man's world! A hard world! It takes a hard, practical man to gain a position of power! I have the money to open doors, to pave the way, and Richard has the brains and looks to become the greatest in the land, and by God!"—he pounded the table again with his fists, his face congested with color—"he's going to get there—in spite of women like you, who want to turn him into a soft, spineless fool!"

"He's only a boy of seven," she gasped.

"I know how old he is, Miss Catherine March!" he replied with icy sarcasm. "And it's never too soon for disciplined training! The world doesn't reward you for kindness. It kicks you in the bottom!"

She stared at him, shaken and incredulous that a man of his education and intelligence could actually believe that kindness and compassion were drawbacks to greatness. And he's jealous, too, because Richard likes me and laughs with me. He can't share the one thing he loves in this world with anyone! "I know my history, Sir James," she said, making a valiant effort to keep the anger out of her voice, "and every great man achieves that greatness because he has a special quality of humaneness . . . a love . . . or compassion for his fellowmen. Other men are remembered for their greed, their brutality." He opened his mouth, and she raised her voice as she raced to finish conveying her thought before he interrupted, "And they usually come to a violent end!"

"Words!" he shouted. "Worthless, simpering, woman-weak words!" He flung his arms out, knocking over the glasses, and the wine spread over the table. She could see Thomas hovering in the background, afraid to come forth unless summoned. "Thomas!" he shouted, and Thomas scurried in and hurriedly cleaned up the sodden mess, shaking his head at her behind the laird's back. Don't say any more, his eyes seemed to say.

Thomas' silent warnings brought her to her senses. She was accomplishing nothing by argument. It wouldn't change the laird's mind and he might force her to leave now if she persisted in crossing him. She turned to make peace with him. He was glaring at her, sullen and vicious.

"Get out of my sight, you green-eyed witch! Go! There's something about you I don't trust, but I'll find it! Never fear, I'll find it!"

She got up from her seat and forced herself to look at him without flinching. "Richard is your son, Sir James. I will follow your wishes, whatever they are."

His eyes narrowed with suspicion at her sudden acquiescence, and their stares were locked. "Very well," he growled at last. "You are to teach my son at his lessons. That's all!"

She nodded mutely, then said, "May I ask one favor?"

"That depends."

"May we ride together occasionally? I'm a stranger to the islands and he's a fine horseman."

"Mmmmm." He grunted. "Well . . . occasionally." He smiled deprecatingly. "That's enough of a man's sport that you can't harm him."

"Thank you," she said stiffly. "Good night, sir." And she held her head high as she walked from the room, wearing her pride like a tattered shirt that didn't quite conceal the wounds of his tongue-lashing.

"Pssst! Miss Catherine!" Richard beckoned her into his room. "Quick!"

She went in, but stood by the closed door. "I can't stay, Richard, I—"

"I heard it all," he broke in. "When my father started shouting, I sneaked down and listened at the Laird's Lug." He grinned. "It's very convenient." His smile faded and he put a hand on her arm. "It's all right, Miss Catherine. We'll be friends. And we'll be able to ride often. Elton told me that they will be away frequently for a week or two at a time. The clans are gathering. It has to do with King Henry's dissolution of some of the monasteries and his declaring himself head of the Church in Great Britain. The Scots will fight him."

Catherine smiled at him, her throat tight. "I'm glad," she said softly. As she went down the hall to her room, she could hear muffled shouts and the sound of breaking things. Her hated grandfather driven mercilessly to violence by his own private demons! And what were his demons? Pain for his dead son, the first Richard? Anger and shame for his idiot son? Guilt and remorse for his slaughter of the Clan MacRaeggan? Surely he felt guilt for his heinous deed and fear for the punishment of God! What about punishment for the sin you are about to commit? It's a sin against God to take another's life! "No!" she cried aloud, leaning against the door, trying to close her ears and mind to her unwelcome thoughts. "I won't think about it! I don't care if it's a sin! I don't care what my punishment is!" But, as she fell in and out of restless sleep, she kept seeing the love in young Richard's face and shining eyes whenever his father voiced the least approval. "I don't care!" she cried, pounding the pillow in her torment. "He's better off without him! He is! He is! He'll only make him hard and brutal—in his own image!"

CHAPTER NINE

The days quickly passed into weeks and the Isles, warmed by the Gulf Stream, swelled into an early spring awakening. Tender green leaves burst from tight, sticky buds, and the sea rolled and rippled in dazzling opalescent shades of blues and greens. The curlew's call hung high and sweet in the sunlight, a different sunlight than Catherine had ever seen. There was an unearthliness about it, and over all was the salty tang of the sea, and the smell of new, wild thyme. But it was the spring twilight that made her heart fairly ache with its exquisite beauty. It had the iridescent pink flush of the inside of a conch shell and it turned the snowcapped mountain peaks a pale rose.

The laird frequently visited the schoolroom, and stayed just long enough to satisfy himself that his son was making rapid progress. When he was in his father's presence, Richard was polite but distant toward Catherine, but his eyes danced with mischief whenever she caught his glance, as if he enjoyed playing this game. The laird was away three or four days at a time, on personal or clan business, and then Catherine and Richard were like two prisoners just granted their freedom. They took special treats to Graham in the tower, and Richard taught him a game with knuckle bones and showed him how to play with a ball made of a pig's bladder. Now when they left the giant would whimper and wail, and Catherine dreaded hearing these sounds that followed them all the way down the tower stairs and echoed in her ears the rest of the night, but his happiness when they came the next time made up for the sadness.

The two friends rode through the golden afternoons, exploring the island, and even on rainy days Catherine found it a magical place. Then she would turn around on her horse and sit there awhile, looking back at the castle, and the gentle, misty rain softened the harsh lines of the fortress and the jagged crags, giving it all a muted watercolor look, fairylike in its delicacy. These were happy hours, and she hugged them to her, savoring every precious moment, knowing they must soon come to an end. She often thought how ironic it was that her daily, civilized routine of living went mindlessly on while her ugly, violent thoughts led a life of their own. She had a plan now, after abandoning one after another as impossible because someone was always with the laird, day and night. Her only hope was to put the lethal drug into the carafe at the side of his bed. Once he drank it there was no hope for him, but it took three or four hours before the pain hit, and then only minutes after that. At this point she always felt sick with revulsion, but she had to harden her heart and mind to the idea. The time period would give her a chance to get to Castle Gullhaven and hide herself and Dileas in the secret room underneath the kitchen floor. Lord Birchmont had told her about it. But, first, she had to visit Castle Gullhaven—see it for herself, familiarize herself with the route she would travel and the way she would cross the Sound of Mull. So there was a lot to do!

It was a glorious fresh, clear day when Richard agreed to take her to see the ancient, abandoned Castle Gullhaven, as he had promised. The laird had left for Carlisle again, with Elton and a few expert bowmen, and they knew it was safe to explore for several days. Thomas and the servants now aided and abetted their adventures by their silence, and thus far no word of their escapades had reached the master's ears. As they rode over the hillocks and dales of the glens, the streams were in full spate, roaring and tumbling like rivers over the rocks, the spray flying high and wild. Richard knew the men who farmed the small crofts, grazing their sheep on rocky pastures that offered slim croppings between patches of heather and bracken, and he told Catherine of their families as they went. They passed neat wattle-and-daub homesteads, pleasantly whitewashed and comfortably tucked in by surrounding barns and byres, their heather-thatched roofs held in place with rocks. Doves fluttered in and out of the dovecotes, and occasionally they saw a burly man and his barefoot son stacking the peat in careful squares against the barns. They waved and called out to them, and once in a while she saw Richard's gaze wistfully follow the actions of a boy near his age, and she felt a fierce resentment that his father had denied him this important part of his boyhood.

Ahead, across the Sound of Mull, bright sunlight flooded the basalt cliffs of Morven, and Catherine could see the pale green leaves of the small trees embracing the cliffs, and the gulls were white wings against the dark stone. Farther out in the blue, guillemots and puffins effortlessly soared and fell with the air currents, and she wished she had wings and could follow them. The horses picked their way carefully around impassable thickets of bog myrtle, heather, and wind-stunted oak and rowan as they worked their way down to the beach on the shallower side of the island, where Richard said a ferry crossed the Sound twice weekly.

The water was high and swift, and the spray stung her cheeks and soaked through her leather jerkin and leather boots, but it only added to her sense of growing excitement as the ferry neared the Morven shore. It was a gentler island, and high above she could see wooded acres: scraggly-limbed junipers, neatly pointed larches, taller rowans, and a splash of beech, red against the darker Scotch pines.

"I'm hungry, Miss Catherine," Richard called out as she paid the ferryman and prepared to mount her horse.

Her first impulse was to push on, to tell him to wait until they had seen Gullhaven, but perhaps it would be better if she put some food into her churning stomach. "All right, Richard. This is a lovely spot, right here on the beach."

"Oh, good! I hope Thomas packed some chicken and some of those plum tarts!" he said as he hurriedly unpacked the saddlebag.

They sat side by side on the white beach of soft, minute grains of shell sand, many feet deep, their backs against a huge rock, their faces to the sea. The sky was like turquoise, and the rolling, tumbling waves were peacock blue, tipped with frothy white, as they broke on the line of jagged rocks and formed quiet miniature pools around the inner circle, making homes for lovely small water creatures: sea anemones, starfish, and sand crabs that climbed out and scuttled along the beach and dug themselves into the soft sand faster than Richard could catch them. A heron stood motionless in the shallows, then with a swift, jabbing motion of its long, needle-sharp bill it impaled a fish and flipped it expertly down its throat. Only she and Richard seemed to exist with the small wild, free creatures. Catherine closed her eyes and lifted her face to the warmth of the sun and felt the soothing fingers of the gentle breeze. How I wish I could make time stand still and could remain a part of this incredible beauty and peace forever, she thought achingly. It would be my sanctuary against the staring, whispering world, unfriendly to those who are different, who were born of tainted parentage!

They rode up above the beach, across the *machair*, a place of coarse sea grasses, sprinkled with tiny, almost hidden wild flowers and stretches of heather, where snow was held in the small crevices. Until now, when it watered the delicate waxen marsh marigolds, the bright yellow crowsfoot, and sometimes the exquisite lilylike asphodel. A family of moorhens popped up and scurried deeper into the bracken, and beyond them one hare and then another leaped and dodged and disappeared in the brush. When they entered the woods, the soft, damp air brought to mind wet leaf mold, moss, crystal-clear water edged with pungent mint . . . the magical wooded spot where William had declared his love and plighted their troth with the beautiful ruby and pearl ring she had left behind with her letter of good-bye. She had tried so long and so desperately to expunge from her mind every word of love he'd spoken, every feature of his beloved face, but it was impossible. She gave a smothered cry and closed her eyes against the pain in her heart. William was like a fever in her blood, from which she would never recover, and its violence would increase through the years, until the heart and soul of her would be burned out, leaving only a mindless shell.

The horses hooves made little sound on the carpet of moss and needles, but it was enough to send a trio of black satin crows, perched on the branches of a dead tree, flapping away, complaining in raucous cries about the intruder.

"That's a bad omen . . . when those black birds come in threes," Richard said as he crossed himself. "It means there will be three deaths within a time of threes: three days or three weeks or three months."

"I don't believe those old superstitions!" she replied hastily, but her breath caught in fear. She wasn't so sure that superstitions, incantations, and rites were to be dismissed lightly. If Richard could read her mind . . . know her diabolical plan . . . how stunned, how horrified this small boy would be!

"Well, cross yourself anyway, Miss Catherine!" he insisted. "You better be safe than sorry!"

"Oh, very well, Richard." And she somehow felt relieved when she complied.

As they reached the edge of the woods, a red squirrel poked its head out of a hole in a tree, skittered to the ground, and came toward them, chipping constantly, stopping now and then to flick its tail and scold a little harder, its beady little eyes full of curiosity. They reined in their mounts and remained motionless until its attention was caught by another squirrel, and they were off on a wild and reckless game of tag, scampering through the leaves, up the trees, leaping from branch to branch. They exploded with laughter, and for a moment Catherine forgot everything but her delight at their crazy antics. But only for a moment . . .

The sound of their laughter sent a tall, spare figure whirling around and then turned her to stone. The woman was clutching a dead rabbit by the ears as she stood in the middle of the rocky clearing.

"She's poaching," Richard whispered.

"Who is she?" Catherine murmured under her breath as they kept riding slowly toward the old woman, who wore a tattered plaid over her head and around her shoulders.

"I don't know. I've never seen her before."

"Hello . . ." Catherine called.

The woman drew herself up, a thin, pitifully proud figure. "*Failte!*" Then, as if aware she was in no danger from the young woman and small boy, she leaned over and dropped the rabbit in a cloth knapsack and tied it around a stout stick, which she put over her shoulder. They were within a few feet of her when she gave a sharp frightened bleat, staring from Richard to Catherine as if she'd suddenly seen ghosts. Her body had a boneless, decentralized lack of coordination as she ran, scrambling over the tumble of huge boulders. As they watched, speechless, they saw her stumble and fall, with a wild flailing of her outstretched arms. Richard reached her first. She was grunting and gasping, trying to free her foot caught between two rocks. She ignored his offer to help, working frantically, twisting and turning. Finally she sagged back into a patch of scree with a dazed, frightened look.

"Togaibh na clachan, leanabh gille!"

"What is she saying, Richard?" Catherine asked as she kneeled down to help.

"She is telling me to 'lift the stone, boy,' " he answered with a grunt as they pushed and tugged, and finally they moved it enough to free her foot. She popped to her feet, then sank down with a moan and a mumbling of Gaelic.

"Please . . ." Catherine soothed. "Sit still. We mean you no harm. Let me look at your foot." She stood quietly as the woman considered. She was not as old as she had thought at first glance. Red still showed in her faded hair, twisted back into a hard knot, visible now that the hood of her plaid had fallen back. But her face was rather odd. It had a fallen look, as if the bones had dissolved and left the skin to hang, unsupported, drawing down the corners of her mouth and pale blue eyes.

"Who . . . air ye?" Her voice wobbled.

"My name is Catherine March. I'm from London, and I am the teacher of the young Richard MacOrvan, here."

"Catherine . . ." The crone's pale eyes fastened on her face like limpets. "I knew a Catherine . . . a Lady Catherine she was, but ye dinna look sae like her, then. It's y'r eyes—y'r green eyes—that hae me worrit!"

Catherine was consumed with excitement. She wanted to question her, but couldn't because of Richard. She shook her head firmly. "I was born and raised in England. My mother was a lady . . . Lady Gwendolyn March. She's dead now, so is my father . . ."

She nodded, as if finally accepting the fact, and made one more effort to stand up but collapsed wincing with pain. She nodded again. "Aye, thankee, lass. 'Twas twisted a bit, nae doot." A low moan escaped her colorless lips as Catherine drew off the rough wet boot, ragged over the toes. Her stocking, cut from wool cloth on the diagonal, was heavily mended but clean. The ankle was swelling rapidly, but as far as she could tell, with gentle probing, there were no broken bones.

"Where do you live? We'll have to help you home."

"Ha nyall! Ha nyall!" She shook her head emphatically. "Ah'll jus' be a usin' me stick, lass, thankee."

Catherine tore off a piece of the picnic cloth and bound the ankle firmly, while Richard sat on a boulder, watching. "What is your name?"

The woman seemed to shrink back into herself as she stared at the boy, and she was muttering under her breath. "Ma name is nae matter," she said at last, taking her stick and putting it under her arm for support, then got to her feet and tried to walk. Catherine caught her as she started to fall and sat her down on a rock. In spite of the gentle breeze a line of heavy perspiration beaded her forehead and her face was white and drawn.

"You'll have to lean on me, and Richard can help you up on my horse. He'll take your knapsack, and I'll ride behind you."

The woman's fear showed plainly on her face. Finally a helpless acquiescence. "I dinna *live* here aboots. Ah'm bidin' for a bit at a sartain place. Deserted it is, sae I do it nae harm. But"—she nodded toward Richard and a brief pain showed in her eyes—"but him that's the laird's bairn . . . he'll be atellin' . . . and the laird'll be a drivin' me awa' . . . or killin' me . . . ."

"Gullhaven!" Catherine guessed in a hushed voice. What else could it be? A deserted place that belonged to Sir James MacOrvan through . . . murder.

The crone nodded, lips twisted in bitterness. "Aye, Gullhaven!" Her head jerked around and she stared at her. "Ye ken Gullhaven, then?"

"No, I've never seen it," she assured her hastily. "Richard told me it belonged to his father, that it was deserted; and he was taking me to see it now."

The old woman shook her head and muttered something about "green eyes" under her breath as the trio stood up on a rock and the two hoisted her up on Dileas, then Catherine got on in front and told her to put her arms around her waist.

The faint footpath twisted high and narrow along a shelf. On one side the sea crashed on the rocks far below; on the other side the broken jumble of basalt cliffs rose sheer above them. The surefooted horses hugged the cliffside and Catherine looked straight ahead. It seemed to her they were climbing up to the pinnacle of the world. The castle grew out of a rocky promontory of thrusting cliffs jutting out over the sea. The castle was similar to Castle MacOrvan, with the same high, thick walls, corner towers, arched gateways, and massive battle nen but it had been built of a pinkish stone which had soft, vitreous sheen to it. That, and the large, lance-headed window and conical, more delicate spires, gave it the arrogant magnificence of a handsome woman irreversibly disintegrating with age.

They finally reached the top of the cliff, and Catherine and Richard got down from their horses to give them a breathing spell. The crone sat still, watching them intently. Directly in front of the castle a narrow path zigzagged down the side of the cliffs to the shore below, where a white sandy beach was ringed with gigantic ragged rocks, which caught the angry lash of the booming breakers and left the little beach at peace. In between the crash of the waves Catherine could hear the sound of the seals, somewhere out on the lonely skerries, singing their eerie songs.

She looked up at the castle. In spite of its sun-softened glow it had a brooding sense of remoteness: the mysterious waiting silence of ancient stone. Eighteen years! It had happened eighteen years ago! A chill ran through her as her mind pictured the horrendous scene: the tough, hard-bitten MacOrvan clansmen, their dark, fierce faces alight with excitement, sneaking up the path along the precipice and swarming silently over the hills to surprise the Clan MacRaeggan at their festive banquet. When they knew their surprise was assured, their spine-chilling war cry broke from their throats and they beat on their targes with the flats of their swords as they rushed the castle.

As if subdued by the great ghostly place, the two wordlessly mounted and rode on up the grassy hill that was splashed with bright daisies and runnelled with gurgling streams edged with the long-stalked royal fern. The drawbridge was closed, and time-battered heraldic beasts, carved in stone, guarded the entrance. At the crone's direction they concealed their horses in a wooded area near the outside walls, then helped her through a broken place in a side wall, so well hidden by a heavy hawthorn brake, no one would guess its existence.

An agonized scream escaped Catherine's lips as she entered the huge courtyard, overgrown with grasses and brambles and filled with the hum of bees hovering over the rough-headed daisies. She stood as if paralyzed, the back of her hand against her mouth, staring horrified at the bleached skulls still impaled, here and there, on those spikes which had gone clear through the head and held the bony remains in place. Her eyes moved in terrified reluctance to take in the grisly heaps of whitened bones and skeletons around the court and the skulls that had fallen from the spikes. She shuddered and collapsed against a wall, hiding her eyes. Her heart thudded crazily and rivulets of perspiration appeared on her face. She felt the tug of Richard's hand.

"Miss Catherine! Miss Catherine! Are you all right?"

She took deep, steadying breaths and slowly straightened up. "Yes. Yes, I'm all right." He was looking up at her anxiously, but there was a pinched, drawn look to his face that wasn't from concern over her. "Have you . . . ever been here before, Richard?"

"No." His eyes swept the gruesome scene and she saw his shoulders convulse with an involuntary shiver. "No. I've ridden around it." His eyes returned to hers. "And I heard about the battle." Battle? Murder, you mean, she shrieked silently. "It was about eighteen years ago, Thomas said, and my father"—he shifted uncomfortably from one foot to the other—"closed it up. No one is allowed to come here. It's supposed to be haunted."

The crone indicated with a bony finger where she wanted to go. They made a chair of hands clasped on each other's arms, to carry her through a servants' entrance, down the stairs to a large kitchen, much the same as that of the MacOrvan castle, but there were two small windows up near the ceiling that let in enough light to see. The place was clean, and a black pot suspended over a small peat fire in the huge fireplace sent out whiffs of steamy goodness. They sat her down on a bench alongside the table and she skinned and gutted the rabbit with dispatch and gave it to Richard to add to the pot. A good supply of peat squares were stacked high on the wall, next to a pile of blankets which made a comfortable bed, and herbs were drying from rafters and heaped on shelves, so she'd evidently been occupying the place for weeks, possibly months. A huge gray cat padded cautiously into the kitchen, snatched the pile of rabbit offal, and streaked to a corner, where he guarded his prize and shrieked in a howl at Richard when he tried to pet him.

"Wheest! Ye'll be gettin' y'r eyes scratched out, then, laddie!" she warned, speaking for the first time since they had entered the castle. "He's fra a wildcat mither and he'll stand nae hand but mine!" She hopped to a stool in front of the fire, with the help of her stick, and stirred the pot, then sat back, gathering her rusty black skirts around her and settling the old faded red and blue plaid around her shoulders. "Weel, laddie, and will ye be a tellin' y'r laird aboot the *cailleach* ye saw this day?"

Catherine had picked up enough Gaelic words to know *cailleach* meant old woman, and when Richard didn't speak, indecision still on his face, she said, "Why don't you tell us about yourself and why you think the laird will drive you away, or kill you? Richard is an honest, fair young man, and if you're honest with him, he'll treat you fairly."

The *cailleach* regarded the two apprehensively, then finally she shrugged, as if to say she had no choice. "Ah'm Siubhan Stewart . . . Judith Stewart . . . *piuthar* o' Thomas . . . sister of Thomas— your Thomas," she translated for Catherine. "I wis midwife o' the MacOrvans sae mony years!" She shook her head in sad recall. " 'Twas I who brang the first Richard, and mony ither bairns, to the

light o' day! Then"—she stopped and her fallen-away face tightened
in a frown as she crossed herself—"then . . . I wis called by the
laird—out o' a sickbed meself—f'r the birthin' o' . . . Graham
MacOrvan. . . ." Her voice trailed away and Catherine heard Richard's gasp. He was leaning forward on his stool, his blue eyes fastened on her face. "The ither midwife hae doon her best. 'Twere too
late to turn him aboot, so he wis birthed feet first, wi' a cord aboot
his neck. And them birthed that way is . . . *daft!*" Her skinny arms
flapped around helplessly, as if trying to push away the inevitable,
then her hands fell into her lap and lay there like two lifeless
lumps. She sighed heavily. "Graham wis twa years, aboot, when
they ken he wis daft. The laird said I hae cast an evil spell, that I
wis a witch and would be burned at the witches' stone. They
burned anither in me place, ane who hae already slippit awa'. But
the laird didna ken aboot it. 'Tis a secret well kept, these years that
I hae been livin' in Inverness. But, Ah'm auld . . . a *cailleach*. I
couldna stay awa' nae longer. I want to dee and be burrit here in
the Isles . . . me hame. . . ." She stared at Richard long and hard.
"Ah'm nae witch, yang Master MacOrvan. I hae *the sight*, but I hae
niver used it fare evil!"

He returned her stare, and at last he nodded. "I shan't tell my father. It will be our secret."

The crone's face worked furiously for a moment, then she murmured, "May God bless you, yang Richard, f'r y'r kindness." And
Catherine felt her own heart expanding with love for this unusual
young man while, conversely, she felt a violent paroxysm of hatred
for his father, whose every crime was calculated and free of remorse.

Richard and Catherine almost reluctantly explored all the rooms
in the main keep. They had come to see Gullhaven and they felt
they must see it all. There were skeletons in all the rooms on the
main floor, some still clothed, just as they had fallen in battle or perhaps been moved a slight degree by foraging animals. Overturned
furniture had never been righted, and sagging draperies, moved
by an unseen breeze, fluttered tattered, ghostly fingers at them. The
bedrooms on the second and third levels were strangely untouched
because everyone must have been at the banquet. Moldering, rotting

clothes still hung in the clothespresses, or on wall hooks; the beds were still made. Small animals had gutted the bolsters, and feathers lay thickly over the floors. To Catherine, moving through these massive rooms—redolent of savage crimes and uneasy spirits—the supernatural took on a different, all-encompassing dimension. She could *feel* her dead clansmen walking at her side with soundless steps, whispering in her ears . . . even her mother. She was sure she had found her room. The gowns looked to have once been light and carefree in their loveliness, just as she imagined her mother's to have been. She longed to examine the small personal belongings more closely, but hesitated to do so with Richard there. She would have to come here again sometime, without him.

When they returned to the kitchen, the *cailleach* was eating a plate of rabbit stew, which she offered to share with them. They declined the stew but shared some of her beastie cheese, which was made from the cow's first milk after she had born a calf, and tasted of a rich egg custard. This old crone has been stealing milk from someone's cow, Catherine thought with amusement, as she finished the last bit on her rough wooden trencher. Then she got up and brought all necessities within convenient reach, so the *cailleach* wouldn't have to hobble too far.

"*Co as a thainig sibh,*" she whispered with a surreptitious glance at Richard, who was at the far side of the kitchen, fashioning a crutch for her from a Y-shaped branch of a small tree. She could put it under her arm and move about easier. "Where do you come from?" she asked again.

"From . . . London . . ." Catherine began.

She shook her head impatiently. "Ye air a MacRaeggan . . . y'r eyes . . . *uaine suilean* . . . green eyes, the shape of y'r nose, y'r mouth . . . the hatred in y'r face at the sight of y'r dead clansmen! Ye air a MacRaeggan, from somm'air!" Catherine opened her mouth but shut it as Richard hurried over, anxious to have the woman try out the stick, which suited her perfectly. But the words of the *cailleach* haunted her for the next few days. If the old woman saw it so clearly, how could Sir James MacOrvan be deceived?

The next few days Catherine kept as busy as her racing thoughts.

There was a new priest in the chapel, and so, for the first time since she had come to Castle MacOrvan, she and Richard heard Matins in the morning and daily Mass. She still couldn't bring herself to go to Confession, and she avoided Father Timothy's gentle reminders as much as possible. The morning studies went on as usual, and they paid their daily visit to Graham in the tower and rode around the island; sailed a small boat on Loch na Keal, and even returned to Gullhaven once, to check on the *cailleach* and take her a few supplies of flour, sugar, ale, and fresh milk, for which she mumbled fervent thanks in Gaelic. But Catherine still had no opportunity to talk to her alone, and when she hobbled out into the courtyard and watched them until they disappeared through the hole in the wall, she could feel her pale blue suspicious eyes boring through her back. It had been a day of uncertain, cloud-scurrying weather, and as she looked through the air filmed with a slight mist, everything took on a translucent, floating quality. The gulls shrieked and complained as they swooped around the cliffs—restless harbingers of an approaching storm—and now she knew how the castle came to be named Gullhaven.

Evenings she kept to her room working on the rich blue wool tunic she was making for Richard's eighth birthday, the 28th of April. It was to have soft leather lacings up the front, and Thomas had mysteriously secured them for her, murmuring his thanks for keeping the secret of his sister, Judith, as he placed them in her hands. At exactly eight o'clock of every evening she watched the lights go up the tower, and then down, as the guards and Thomas took Graham out for his exercise in the courtyard. The servants were safely in their rooms, on the third level of the main keep or in the outer buildings, and the laird—when he was in residence—was well into his cups, unaware or uncaring of his idiot son's presence.

Sir James arrived on the morning of Richard's birthday. It was a brilliant, freshly washed morning, filled with excitement as the castle seethed with preparations for the mammoth feast and celebration. It was to be a double one because the laird's fifty-eighth birthday was two days after that of his son, so they celebrated their birthdays together. Families came from everywhere, rich and poor, noble and peasant, and Catherine found it a colorful scene, with a mind-boggling hodgepodge of dress. She was fascinated by the variety of homespun tartan plaids. Most of the wealthy ones wore the striking highland dress of kilt and plaid, and in their bonnets their clan badge: a sprig of yew or oak, bog myrtle or cranberry. At their waists a claymore, or a small halbert—a large dagger sharpened on one side—or a longbow and arrows slung over their shoulders. There were long tunics and trews, sheepskin coats, and the poorer Highlander often wore his plaid as his complete dress, over one shoulder and belted into kilts, leaving his arms and legs bare. The women wore saffron or gray dresses, with a plaid over their shoulders which could be used as a blanket if the weather turned chill, except for the ladies of the different lairds who wore rich gowns under their plaids and gold chains and jewels around their necks.

Sir James and Richard were the handsomest father and son there, and her eyes kept straying back to them, and she had to breathe deeply to break the heavy bands that seemed to constrict her chest. Her grandfather had had short coats and kilts of the MacOrvan plaid tailored for him and his son, and with them they wore tartan stockings to the knees and fine white linen shirts. King James V had adopted this style for his hunting costume, and the nobles quickly followed the fashion trend. Why does it have to be this way? she screamed silently. Why do you have to be the diabolical murderer you are? I could have been so proud of you as a man, a leader, but something is warped in you that lets you commit terrible deeds without remorse!

The games and feasting went on all day, and the kegs of ale and wines were constantly replenished. Catherine joined in the tug-o'-war and the races, and she watched, enthralled, as a tall, muscular giant won the cabertossing for the Clan MacOrvan by picking up the big tree trunk and tossing it completely over, so it lay in a straight line from his body. Richard was in his element. There were many boys near his age, and he bested them in every competition, from target shooting to hammer throwing and racing, and his father roared his approval, his blue eyes alight with fierce pride.

The dancing began as the breathtaking amethyst twilight was

falling: the Highland Fling, the intricate Sword Dance, the Reel of Tulloch, and many others that Catherine wasn't familiar with. It was while she was watching Sir James and Richard in a beautiful execution of the Sword Dance that she happened to turn and saw the oddly assembled face of Judith Stewart at the side of her. A gasp escaped her lips and the *cailleach* shook her head in a silent warning, then leaned over and whispered in her ear, "Niver fear, lass, Ah'm anly anither *cailleach* in sae mony folk! The laird wouldna ken the likes o' me noo. 'Tis the anly chance to see the castle and me family."

Catherine breathed easier. It was probably true. She had left some thirty-four years ago, and now she was just another old woman with a plaid over her head, in a crowd of many. "But don't take a chance. Keep out of the laird's way . . . and Elton's," she added as an afterthought. The old woman nodded and melted into the mass of people.

The flames of the bonfires leaped higher, the dancing grew wilder and the laughter and talk more boisterous. Catherine looked around cautiously. She had seen Thomas, Elton . . . all the house servants. Everyone was here, outside. Now was her chance to slip the poison into the carafe at the laird's bedside. She made her way slowly through the crowds, to the side entrance of the keep, stopping to say a word here, to watch a dance there, and finally she slipped inside and raced up the stairs. She stood before his door and tried to bring her hand up, willing her mind to twist the handle, but she seemed curiously atrophied and just stood there, unwilling to stay, unable to find the courage to leave. You fool! You silly fool, open it! she told herself angrily. He slaughtered all your people and had your mother ravished! You vowed vengeance! Now keep your promise! She tried the door and her heart gave a jolt. Was it from disappointment, or was she glad to find it locked? She tried it again, automatically, and it opened slowly, unwillingly. It had only been stuck! A lamp was burning at the side of the bed, and a prickling of fear moved over her scalp. It's always lighted at dusk when the laird is here, she reminded herself nervously.

For a moment she forgot her lethal mission as she stood looking around the room. How strange! It was a spartan room, monklike in its severity: a large crude bed, a clothespress, and two stools. No tapestries, no pictures, nothing to show a man of education, wealth, and a taste for luxury lived here. What were those? Pictures turned to the wall? She moved like a sleepwalker to turn one over and gave a muffled exclamation. A mirror! She turned the other two. Mirrors! He turned his mirrors to the wall! Why? Ah, yes! Yes! She remembered the superstition: If a man has the soul and heart of a devil, the devil will look out of his reflection! So he knew what he was!

She was suddenly conscious of her own reflection. She hadn't seen herself clearly for months, and somehow she had expected to look older . . . more harried . . . with a stamp of guilt on her face, but the girl who looked back at her appeared just the same except for the hair coloring, which seemed oddly out of place. She gave a low cry of dismay as she peered closer. Her headdress had slipped awry and there was a wide black silken line at the roots of her hair where it was parted in the middle! She had redyed her hair once after her arrival at Castle MacOrvan, but she'd been so preoccupied these past weeks she'd given it no thought and she'd used up all the dye! She forced her frantic thoughts into coherent order. I can part it on the side and bring some of the long front hair across the hairline. The headdress will hide the crossing. But then . . . why will I have to hide it? The deed will be done! The laird will not come to his bed until late and he will be too drunk to notice any difference in the taste of the ale in the carafe. I will slip away. The guards will be in a stupor, too, and no one will be guarding the entrance. The ferryman was hired by the laird for all-night duty, so he will be there to take me across. But he will tell! They will know I'm on Morven and somewhere in Castle Gullhaven! They won't rest until they have hunted me down! All right, then that plan must be discarded. I'll have to take the small boat moored on Loch na Keal and make my way to Iona, where I will ask for sanctuary. No . . . She shook her head silently, still staring in the mirror, watching her face settle into sober lines of resignation. I will have to stay. There are many men here who come in friendship but who hate Sir James.

Any one of them could be guilty of poisoning him. But if one in particular is accused, I will have to admit my guilt.

She turned unwillingly and walked slowly to the bed and stood looking down at it, her mind's eye picturing her grandfather lying there, screaming and twisting in gruesome agony as the poison ate away his insides! She was stabbed with an intense cold that only terror can produce, and she couldn't quiet the trembling of her hands as she tried to remove the stopper from the bottle. Would his suffering be any more intense than what he went through every day and night of his life? He was driven by his own demons to drown his guilt in drink, to shout and smash things. He turned his mirrors to the wall because he couldn't bear to see his devil's soul! The stopper was out and she held the bottle over the large stone one that held the ale. She closed her eyes as a wave of nausea passed over her. Now Richard's sweet young face was burned into her eyelids, sweeping everything else out of her mind. How he would hate and despise her for violating his trust and his friendship! Richard loved his father deeply. He was bright enough to see his shortcomings, and to live with them, but they didn't lessen his love. What would his violent death do to a sensitive young boy? How would it affect him? She opened her eyes. How dare you play God? she asked herself incredulously. How dare you deliberately bring pain and sorrow to an innocent young boy just to satisfy your own hurt? It wouldn't bring the MacRaeggans back to life! It would only satisfy your need for vengeance!

She was abruptly aware that her hand was shaking violently and the poison was pouring down into the ale. Her eyes widened in panic as she stared, hypnotized. "No! No!" she moaned. "You have no right to exact your own punishment by taking another's life! Only God gives life, only God has the right to take life! He will be punished by God!" Shuddering with horror, she flung the poison away and knocked over the bottle of ale, then sank to her knees and buried her face against the bed, overcome with tempestuous weeping.

She recoiled with a shriek at the touch of a hand on her shoulder.

Thomas' wizened face looked down into hers and she noticed with a stupid irrelevancy that he still wore the Stewart plaid over his saffron tunic.

"Ye couldna do it, lass, could ye? 'Tis a great hate ye carry in y'r heart!" He sighed and shook his head. "But 'tis God-fearin' folk we air! Och! I'll be a cleanin' it oop, then." He busied himself pouring water from the ewer into the basin and cleaning up the floor, smashing the ale bottle—which made her jump—and wrapping it in a cloth, to be discarded. She watched him mutely, but her thoughts were racing. How long had he been there? How much had he seen?

"I followed ye, lass. Ye'r a MacRaeggan and ye hae the richt to hate! Fra where do ye come, then? Fra wha sept o' the MacRaeggans? Who air ye?" His eyes suddenly widened as he gaped at her hair. "Black! Y'r hair is black! Who *air* ye?" he repeated hoarsely.

"Who do you think I am?"

"Ye hae the spittin' look o' Lady Anne MacRaeggan, but f'r y'r hair, and it's . . . it's . . ." His voice thinned in fear.

She got up and sat on the edge of the bed. "Yes, my hair is black, Thomas," she said bitterly, "black and shiny as the wings of the raven." A gasp gurgled and died in his throat. "My mother was Lady Anne MacRaeggan, and my father is . . . Graham MacOrvan . . . !" The words trailed off in a thin cry of denial.

"*Mo Dia! Mo Dia!*" he whispered, crossing himself. "Hae ye coom back, then, t' carry aout ye mither's curse?"

"My mother's curse. Yes, she did put a curse on him! I saw it once in a ballad they sing: 'I call a curse down on you, James Mac-Orvan, Laird of the Clan MacOrvan! May you know all the tortures of the eternally damned, before you strangle to death in your own blood!' Is that the way it went, Thomas?"

His face was stricken, and he twisted his fingers nervously in the hem of his tunic. "Aye, lass. The laird hae ken the tortures o' his guilt, and of late I hae seen the shroud aboot his feet . . ."

"You have the *sight*, Thomas?"

"Aye, lass."

"Then it must be by some other hand than mine."

"The sight dinna be tellin' me ever' wee thing, lass, anly wha'

Ah'm to ken fra the time, but ye'll see, ye'll see!" They were both silent with their own sober thoughts, then he sighed and said, "The laird wis told Lady Anne slippit awa' in a nunnery."

"Not until after I was born." She paused. "Everyone seems to guess I'm a MacRaeggan. What about Sir James . . . my grandfather?" Her lips twisted wryly.

There was compassion in his pale blue eyes and a look of distress on his simianlike face. "He kens ye'r fra a sept o' the MacRaeggans. He thought pairhaps fra the Ewans. We wis to keep a sharp eye on ye, then, but we didna tell him nae thing!" he added quickly.

"The Ewans. They were the brothers, related to the MacRaeggans, who accused Sir Ronald MacRaeggan of murdering the laird's first son, Richard."

"Aye, but they wis a lyin'!"

Her head snapped up. "How . . . how do you know?"

"Befair they ken they wis to dee"—he ran a finger across his throat —"the Ewans made confession of they lies t' Father Aonghas. He kept silent ontil fower years agae, w'en the laird turned him aout— there wis bad blood a'tween the twa—then Father Aonghas brake his vow o' silence an' screammit the truth." He crossed himself again.

"How the priest must have hated him to commit such a sin against his Holy Orders!" she said, almost to herself. "So"—she looked up at the small bent man—"for four years the laird has known he's the worst kind of a murderer! How can he live with such a guilt? Why did he believe the Ewans?" She pounded the bed with her clenched fists. Why didn't he give the MacRaeggans a chance to deny it . . . and find out the truth . . . instead of just slaughtering them in cold blood?

He shook his head sadly. "Och! Since the day he ken his bairn Graham wis daft, he changeit. Airy bit o' pride, o' love wis bounden oop in Richard! When Richard was killit, he wis like a man daft!" He made a vicious jabbing sweep with his arms. "He dinna hae nae razon . . . he heerd anly wha' he wanted, and he killit . . . and killit!"

She got up feeling completely drained. "I must leave here in a day or two, Thomas. I can better understand the man, but I can never feel anything but a deep and terrible hatred for him, and someday I might try again . . . !"

He nodded. "Aye. But"—he caught her arm and held it with surprising strength—"ye mustna tell him who ye air!"

A cold smile touched the corners of her lips. "No. He wouldn't appreciate the fact that there's another 'tainted' MacOrvan in the world!"

She had no stomach for returning to the celebration, but she was glad she did when Richard told her he'd been searching for her and claimed her as his partner in a sprightly reel. Every time she looked at his glowing face or heard the sound of his happy laughter, she gave silent thanks to God that she had come to her senses in time. The hour was growing late, and although the revelers were still in full swing, the crowd had thinned a little. Some had gone back to their homes, others were asleep, sprawled in the corners of the courtyard, covered with their plaids, their bonnets serving as pillows. Catherine felt completely exhausted from the highly emotional day, and she was about to slip away to her room when Thomas surreptitiously edged close to her.

"Miss Catherine, Ah'm needin' y'r help!" he whispered, his voice sharp with alarm. She stood still, without turning her head. "The laird kens aboot *mo piuthar* . . . my sister. Elton wis heerin' it fra sommone on Morven wha saw her milkin' his cow."

"But the laird won't harm her after all these years!" she protested without turning.

"Aye!" he muttered. "She be a witch to him that's the laird! He'll hae her burned!"

A chill passed over her at the acceptance of such barbarism. "Does he know she's here?"

"*Hanyall!* He'll be sendin' his men to Gullhaven in the mornin', then!"

"Then hide her here!" She heard his barely controlled gasp. "He won't think to look right under his nose. Hide her . . ." Her thoughts rapidly discarded one place after another. "I know; hide her in the dungeon. No one goes there. Since you're her brother, they'll be watching you, Thomas. After everyone's asleep, I'll take her some blankets and food. I'll get Richard to help me." In answer to his grunt she added, "He won't tell. He's kept the secret so far. He keeps his promises." She sensed rather than saw his nod as he walked away, mingling with the press of people who were dancing to the skirl of the bagpipes.

It was the dark thick gray just before dawn when Catherine and Richard stepped out cautiously into the courtyard, their arms full of things for the *cailleach*. The dying bonfires cast just enough glow to enable them to make their way around and over the slumbering revelers. Every time someone stirred or snorted himself awake for a brief moment, her heart sank. At the entrance to the dungeon Richard put his load down and lit the lamp, which cast such a feeble light that Catherine felt as if they were being swallowed by the gaping black mouth.

"*Có tha sinn?*" The faint whisper had overtones of fear.

"It's Richard and Miss Catherine." His voice hit the damp, moldering walls and echoed ahead of them.

"Och! Ye'r a sicht f'r auld eyes!" The *cailleach* grabbed the bucket of ale and drank greedily. "'Tis thirsty I am with all this waitin'!" She wiped her mouth with the back of her hand and belched.

"We got here as soon as we could," Catherine replied testily. "We had to wait until everyone was asleep."

The crone touched her arm, and Catherine looked down at her and was ashamed for the testiness when she saw the anxious smile on her face. "'Tis grateful I am, lass, but 'tis frightened I am, then."

She put an arm around her and hugged her skinny shoulders. "Don't be afraid. He'll never think of looking for you at Castle MacOrvan." The old woman's glance slid to Richard. "He won't tell. The one whose cow you milked told Elton."

"Wheest! I canna thole the man! He's cauld as a puddock!" She hobbled about without her stick as she helped them make a bed of several sheepskins and blankets from Richard's room, and she ate hungrily of the bread and cheese and cold lamb.

"We'll be back maybe tonight, if we can . . . but don't be alarmed if we don't make it. You have enough food until tomorrow," Catherine said before they felt their way back up the long flight of stone stairs and out into the blessed freshness of the early morning air. She sank like a rock into sleep and knew nothing more until Thomas tapped on her door to call her to breakfast. In spite of the late celebration the early lessons were to continue, evidently!

Richard greeted her sleepily, and everyone in the kitchen seemed very subdued, and when Richard said in a low voice, "My father has gone to Morven with Thomas and Elton and ten of his men," she knew why. "He took Prince and King," he continued with a worried frown, his spoon suspended over his porridge as he leaned across the table, "and they'll get something of hers from the kitchen at Gullhaven and have the dogs smell it. That's the way they'll track her." They stared at each other with growing alarm. "What if the dogs track her *here?*"

Between their lack of sleep and worry about the *cailleach* they had difficulty concentrating on Richard's studies, and they welcomed Thomas with enthusiasm when he brought them some cakes and cool fruit juice.

Richard fell asleep, sitting on the floor with his back against the wall, an unfinished piece of cake in his hand. Catherine sat looking at him a long time. The warmth of the morning formed fine black curls across his forehead and down around his ears, his long black lashes lay like a silken fan on his sun-ruddy cheeks, a spattering of dark freckles dusted over a nose that would be straight and arrogant like his father's, but his mouth was still sweet and childishly soft. He was wearing the blue tunic she had made him—and which he declared was his favorite present—and it seemed to give him added breadth across the shoulders. How I'll miss him! she thought with a sting of tears in her throat. She couldn't lift his weight, but she put a pillow on the floor for his head and tipped him gently over. He stirred and mumbled but slept on, and she curled up on a bench and knew nothing more until Thomas shook her awake.

"Wheest, Miss Catherine! 'Tis aboot time f'r supper. The laird'll be a lookin' f'r ye both!"

Every sense was instantly alert. "What happened, Thomas? Did you go to Gullhaven?" He nodded. "Did the dogs . . . ?"

"Aye. The dugs found her tracks f'r a time, but lost them aboot a *larach* on Morven." Lost them near a ruined homestead, she automatically translated.

"Oh, thank goodness!"

His monkey face sobered. "Dinna talk aboot it t' the laird, Miss Catherine. He's fare in his cups and in an oogly tempair! It bides ill f'r all o' us wha gave her help afore."

Catherine carefully redressed her hair—wishing she had a mirror —and put on the mustard-colored gown, trimmed with black braid, remembering how she'd worn it for her first meeting with Lord Birchmont, at St. Clements. How long ago that seemed! She felt better able to handle disagreeable situations when she was well groomed, and from the moment she sat down at the supper table, she knew it was going to be just that. Sir James, adhering to his usual fastidious taste, had changed into full Highland dress that he'd worn for the celebration and that suited his handsome hawkish person more than any other attire. But his face mirrored his dark displeasure and frustration. He had been drinking heavily, and every time Thomas came scurrying in, in answer to his bellow, he glared at him ferociously before he gave him an order, as if he were blaming him personally for their failure to hunt down the *cailleach* and he were planning some dreadful punishment for his old manservant.

The laird was civil but cold to her, and she became increasingly restive under his swift, enigmatical glances. Why didn't he accuse her right out of being a MacRaeggan? Was he still trying to figure out *which* MacRaeggan, or from which sept of the MacRaeggans, or was there some ugly, perfidious reason behind his supposed acceptance of her as Edna Catherine March, nurse and teacher? Was he deliberately trying to lull her fear of discovery to the point where she felt herself safe? Then would he strike? He'd known for four years now that the MacRaeggans were innocent victims of his savage hate, but was his hate so deep a part of him that he couldn't free himself of it? He had sworn death to every MacRaeggan, so would killing another one mean no more than swatting a troublesome midge? How bizarre if they were both plotting the other's death! Every time she looked at him she thought how formidably close she had come to murdering him, and the thought turned her cold. She tried to keep her eyes on her plate, but she found herself staring at him, time and again, drawn and repelled simultaneously, as with a venomous reptile.

It was with a feeling of intense relief that she could finally stop picking and poking at her food and excuse herself to go to her room. He nodded with an impatient lift of one shoulder and glared at her, his bloodshot deep blue eyes glittering dangerously.

My grandfather is mad! she thought as she paced her room in great agitation. Not a noisy madness that could be detected by friends and clansmen—and only those in the main keep are privy to his drunken ravings—but the kind of madness that has given him strength and power to destroy without remorse. His pride of name and family is his madness. Anyone who takes that from him is his enemy and must be destroyed! No weakness can possibly come from him; it's caused by another—an enemy—by a curse, a spell. That's why he won't rest until he finds the *cailleach*, and he'll have her burned at the stake, as a witch, without a whit of remorse! And then Thomas, and all the others who helped her escape years ago, will be punished, one by one, in the name of clan justice!

There was a quick, secretive tap on the door and Richard slid inside and closed it carefully behind him. "Miss Catherine"—he hurried to her side and grasped her hand, his eyes wide with consternation—"my father is talking to Elton about the *cailleach*. I listened at the Laird's Lug. He's sure she's here on Mull, befriended by some of her people. He's sending out men with Prince and King and the bloodhounds."

"When?"

"Tonight."

"Not . . . not in the morning?"

"No. He . . . he thinks the dogs can flush her out easier in the dark . . . when . . . when she can't see her way." He looked on the verge of tears, and Catherine folded him in her arms and they held tightly to each other, without saying a word. Finally she released him.

"Did they mention any time, Richard?"

"Yes. The men are to gather in the courtyard at nine o'clock, with the dogs. They have a coat of the *cailleach*."

"Auugh! That might lead them right to her!" She thought a moment, then took a breath of decision. "You must find Thomas quickly. Tell him to get word to her *somehow* that she's to be at the top of the stairs at dark. She'll just have to wait for us, since she has no way of telling the time. We'll come for her around eight-fifteen."

"But that's the time the guards take Graham out for his exercise."

"They take him out exactly at eight. At eight-fifteen he'll be at the far end of the courtyard, and it will be dusky enough so they can't tell what's going on even if they should look back."

"Where will we hide her?"

"Richard . . . remember how we made a chair of our hands clasped to each other's arms?" He nodded. "Well, if we *carry* her, she won't make *tracks!*" He clapped his hands and muffled a burst of laughter. "Shhhh!" she cautioned. "Then we'll take her up to my room . . . until they can get her away in a boat."

"My room!" he corrected her.

"No, Richard. I don't want your father to know your part in this."

"*My room!*" he insisted stubbornly. "No one would think of looking there."

"Very well," she agreed, with a reluctant sigh.

A heavy evening mist rolled in and wrapped the castle in a soft, moist blanket, making it impossible to see more than a few feet away, and Catherine gave silent thanks for this unexpected help. Sir James was still drinking with Elton, and it would probably go on until the men and dogs assembled.

The two hid in the schoolroom until Graham and his guards went out, accompanied by Thomas, as usual; then they hurried out behind them, peering into the night. Fog flares on either side of the entrance lit up only the immediate area, and they walked cautiously into the wall of thick murk, moving in what they hoped was the right direction. They held hands, and Catherine wasn't sure which one of them was trembling. The fog confused them and they ended up at the chapel, but at least this helped them get their bearings.

They felt their way, hands outstretched; two buildings to the left and the outer keep, with its dungeon, loomed up before them.

"Judith! Are you there? It's Catherine and Richard," she called out *sotto voce,* praying the *cailleach* had their message. There was silence and her heart sank, but then she heard a light scrambling sound.

"Aye! Aye! Where air ye? I canna see!"

"Here! Keep talking low . . . we'll find you." They moved slowly, feeling with their outstretched hands. A wrong move and they could tumble down the open stairs. After what seemed like many precious lost minutes, Catherine felt the clasp of bony fingers that clung to hers in a death grip. She tried, unsuccessfully, to pry them loose. "Judith . . . hold onto my shoulder. We must be quick. Richard and I will make the same chair with our hands."

The old crone did as she was bid, chuckling to herself. "Thomas tol' me wha' ye plan. 'Tis bright ye air! Thankee both."

Don't thank us yet, Catherine said to herself as they swung the light bundle of bones off her feet and started off in what they hoped was a diagonal direction. It wasn't, and she could feel her nerves tighten, and she had to clench her teeth to keep them from chattering. Finally there was the pale glow from the torches ahead, and the relief was so great it made her feel light-headed. Now they dared to pick up their pace until they were almost running. They were within the circle of light! They had made it!

The shock was so abrupt it was like a heavy blow to the body, and they stood there motionless, gaping at the figure of Sir James outlined in the doorway. Behind him stood Elton. He walked with slow deliberation down the three stone steps and came to a halt in front of them. The naked rage in his face was terrifying, and there was a knife-cutting thrust in his low voice: "So . . . we meet again, Judith Stewart . . . cursed witch! This time you won't escape your punishment! I will personally watch you burn as soon as it's daylight! We'll be rid of you and your evil spells once and for all!"

"No, Father! Please! She's not a witch! She's just a harmless *cailleach* who came home to die! Let her go, Father!"

The laird's lips twisted in fury and he struck Richard so hard with the flat of his hand that it knocked him to the ground. "My son!" he screamed. "My own flesh and blood plotting against me!" He raised his hand again and Catherine flung herself against him, hanging onto his arms.

"Stop it! Stop it!"

Elton tore her away and she fell on the wet cobblestones, the breath knocked out of her. "You!" The laird stood over her, shaking his fist in her face. "You led him on! He's only a small boy!" He dragged her to her feet and shook her like a rag doll as she kicked and scratched. "What MacRaeggan are you? Did you come for revenge?" He shook her again.

"Yes! Yes! I'm a MacRaeggan!" she gasped painfully. "Lady Anne MacRaeggan was my mother, and my father is . . . Graham MacOrvan!"

For a moment he was turned to stone, staring at her transfixed, then he released his grip and pushed her away as if she were something unclean. "No!" he bellowed like a crazed bull. "She died!"

"After I was born!" she shrilled.

"*Ha nyall!*" The *cailleach* scrambled up the steps and turned to face them. She raised a hand, one long skeletal finger pointing to the heavens. " 'Tis nae true!" Her thin, shrill voice turned them all to statues of frozen animation as they stared up at the black-cloaked, witchlike figure that seemed to float in and out of the swirling mist. "The lass *air* the daughter o' Lady Anne MacRaeggan, but her faither wis the fairst-born Richard MacOrvan!" She pointed an accusing finger at the laird, who stood gaping at her. "Lady Anne wis wi' child o' y'r fairst Richard when ye brought her t' shame! They wis wed in a hand-fastin' since ye twa clans hae forbid they marriage!"

The laird seemed to be fighting his way out of a stupor. "We agreed to the marriage!" he cried hoarsely.

"Anly w'en it wis too late! Anly after t' hand-fastin'!"

The small seed of hope planted by the *cailleach's* first words now burst into fierce, wonderful blossom, and Catherine stood still, her face raised to the skies, laughing and crying in a wild eruption of joy. A tiny corner of her conscious mind recorded the fact that

Graham MacOrvan was standing at the edge of the light, guards on either side, gazing on the bewildering scene.

With a roar the laird charged the old woman, beating her to the ground and crying out his anguish, "Why did you keep it secret? All these years! My Richard! My granddaughter!"

Catherine sprang on him like a wildcat, shrieking and clawing, and young Richard rushed to hold his father back from the *cailleach*. In his blind rage the laird knocked them both down and the scene became a nightmare of mistbound violence. With a piercing cry of protest—unearthly terrible—Graham broke from his guards, sent Elton crashing to the cobblestones, where he lay in awkward stillness, and leaped on the back of the laird, bearing him to the ground, crushing him with his weight. The giant's eyes were filled with ungodly flames of savagery as he brought his shackled hands down with all his strength onto the laird's throat. He rolled back on his haunches, watching uncomprehendingly as the laird lay dying. He was still watching as the guards rammed their spears into his back. His eyes widened in surprise and he turned slightly, holding his hands out to Catherine and Richard before he fell over on the laird, their blood mingling. In death he embraced his father for the first time.

CHAPTER TEN

Catherine walked barefoot along the shore with Richard. The mud and seaweed squishing between her toes felt satin-soft, the gentle lap of the waves was like music: soothing, soporific. They had walked this white sandy beach, on the Isle of Morven, many times since the violent deaths of the three MacOrvan men, letting its peaceful beauty mend their troubled hearts. But young Richard proved a true, proud MacOrvan, making fair decisions far beyond his years: the *cailleach* was given a comfortable croft with a cow, a goat, and a few sheep and chickens; and Thomas would remain at his side. He didn't ask Catherine to stay in so many words, but his eyes were filled with anxiety until she assured him they would be together until he chose to be on his own.

They came back to their favorite spot and flopped down on the warm sand, their backs against a huge rock, their faces to a sea that looked as smooth as turquoise glass. A soft breeze stirred a tendril of her hair that fell free in a black silken mass onto the white linen tunic she wore over her blue trews. There were only the two of them in this primal solitude, and her eyes drank in its magnificence. The mist-hung mountains of Mull in the distance, the sweep of the white sand against the dark red cliffs that were splashed with bright velvety clusters of yellow primrose, and a hint of emerald green moss in between patches of brownish scree. A golden eagle—arrogant, undisputed king of the skies—wheeled high above the sea cliffs.

Half-formed thoughts floated around in her mind. Her first impulse, when the wonderful truth of her parentage had sunk in, was to fly to William's arms, joyously declaring herself a fit wife for him. But, illogically, it hurt her deeply that his love wasn't strong enough to survive the blow, brutal as it was. Cooler, saner reflection made her realize how unfair, how unrealistic she was. No man would risk bringing such children into the world. Every time he would look into her face he would imagine a look of madness. Nevertheless, the hurt remained to rankle and pain. He was probably married by now because he must have heirs to carry on the lineage.

A gannet hovered above the water and suddenly plunged, wings folded, and came up with a large fish, too heavy for its size. The bird flopped clumsily across the surface of the water, unable to take wing, and finally had to drop its prize. Richard exploded with laughter, and the sound filled Catherine with a deep, restorative sense of peace. How good it was to hear him laugh again!

Richard shook her awake. "Catherine! Someone's coming! Strangers!"

It took her a moment to shake away the drug of sleep, but the sight of the boat turning into shore drove her to her feet, her heart squeezed with sudden agonizing pain. He stood tall in the prow, like a conquering Viking of old. He was hatless, and the afternoon sun formed a nimbus around his golden hair. She stood motionless, waiting, scarcely daring to breathe or to believe what she was seeing.

He jumped out before the boat touched ground and cleared the space between them with long strides, sweeping her into his arms and holding her crushed to his chest. He crooned her name over and over like a litany as he smothered her face, her hair, with kisses: "Catherine! Catherine! My love! My dearest love! Oh, God, how I've longed for you!"

She clung to him in overpowering, laughing ecstasy. "Oh, William! William! William!" She ran her hands over his back, his shoulders, up into his hair. Touching him was like touching an extension of her own body . . . her soul . . . her heart.

He put her gently aside and stood looking down into her face, which was filled with a golden rapture, as if he were seeing an unhoped-for miracle. "I'll never let you go! Never let you out of my sight again," he said ardently. The blue of his eyes deepened and flamed with growing desire, and he molded her into the very flesh of him as his mouth claimed hers, and the fierceness of their love—so long denied—burned in a passion that sent them soaring to dizzying heights of ecstasy. After a time he took her face in gentle hands, his eyes filled with tenderness. "It doesn't matter about your father. It took a long, almost fatal illness to make me realize that! Whatever comes, we'll face it together, my darling! My life has no meaning without you by my side." He smoothed her hair away from her lovely face and smiled.

His words were like a magical, healing balm. She stood on her toes and kissed him passionately on the mouth, then wound her arms tightly around his neck as she whispered, "You promised once that you would keep me constantly 'with child,' and I'm going to hold you to that promise!"

EPILOGUE

Sweet spring hazed the afternoon air, and Catherine felt the familiar excitement of renewal, of new life burgeoning from the rich English soil . . . and the new, precious life she carried again in her body. It had been twenty wonderful years since their first son was born and named William Brooks Lester, after his paternal grandfather. He was a young attorney now, and his wife was soon to give birth. She smiled broadly.

"What do you find so amusing?" Tansy said, putting down her needlepoint and smiling at her dearest friend. She looked like the contented very prosperous matron she was, in a fashionable gown of light blue velvet that made her round gray eyes appear more blue than gray.

"I was just thinking," Catherine answered with a soft chuckle, "that I may be a new grandmother at the same time I'm a mother for the *eighth* time!" She sighed. "How fast the years go! I'm beginning to feel my age . . . for the first time!"

"Oh, pooh! You're young yet . . . only thirty-eight . . . and still as beautiful as ever!" Tansy gave a disbelieving shake of her head as she looked at the lovely woman, gowned in her favorite light green, sitting with her on the sweeping expanse of lawn surrounding Fair Meadows like a park. "And, obviously, your husband still thinks so!" she added with an impish grin.

"And so does yours!" Catherine nodded at Tansy's swelling waistline, and they broke into laughter. "Oh! There they come!" She pointed at a group of riders thundering across the fields toward the lawn, and they stood up to watch the finish of the usual afternoon race. A girl with bright red-gold hair streaming out behind her had the lead, and she recklessly kept it until she brought her mount up short in front of them and jumped off.

"I did it again!" she laughed gleefully as she kissed Catherine on the cheek, and then her "Aunt Tansy," and flopped on the grass.

"Julena . . . the grass is damp. You'll catch your death of cold!" Catherine automatically warned her ten-year-old daughter.

Julena turned the sparkling battery of her beautiful green eyes on her mother and nothing more was said. Julena never had a cold and she always sat where she pleased, and they both knew it.

There was a flurry of laughter and talk as the other riders arrived. William, still lean and golden, kissed his wife and nuzzled her neck with unabashed warmth, while Frank kissed Tansy, and the children gathered around for refreshments, good-naturedly grumbling about Julena's winning streak. They were all healthy, handsome youngsters, and she loved them all dearly, including Tansy's, but Catherine's eyes kept turning to Julena. She was the Scot of the bunch, with the exquisite coloring of Lady Anne, but there was a fire, an arrogance, a will of iron that came from the MacOrvan side. Would there be a man, someday, who could temper it with the strength of his love?

She felt a strange restlessness that always tugged at her in the spring. Then she recalled the beauty of the Isles: the incredible sunsets, the crystal cascades of water, the jewel-like notes of the curlew, the crashing storms . . . and she felt the call of her clansmen. Richard was happy with a growing family at Castle MacOrvan; Thomas and the *cailleach* had "slippit awa'," as had dear Sister Emily and Reverend Mother; Sheila had been married off to Gerald Walker, the physician's son. Gullhaven had long ago been returned to her. Her Uncle Keith wanted no part of it, and she had had it put in some order. But it still waited, high on the rocky cliffs jutting over the sea . . . waited for a MacRaeggan to return. She looked at Julena again. Yes . . . Julena. . . .